DATE DUE

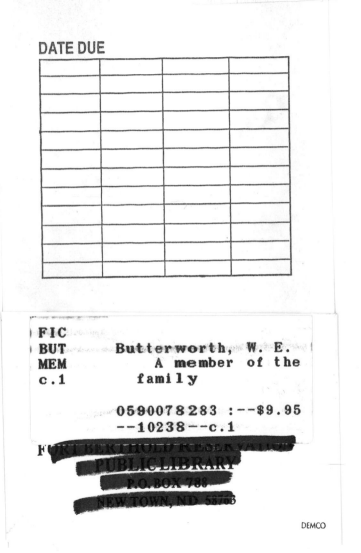

DEMCO

W. E. Butterworth

A Member of the Family

FOUR WINDS PRESS

NEW YORK

067916

LIBRARY OF CONGRESS CATALOGING IN PUBLICATION DATA

Butterworth, W. E. (William Edmund), 1929–
  A member of the family.

  SUMMARY: When a lovable English sheepdog begins to
display vicious behavior at odd times due to psychological
problems caused by inbreeding, his owners are faced with
a heartbreaking decision.
  [1. Old English sheepdog—Fiction. 2. Dogs—Fiction]
I. Title.
PZ7.B9825Me 1982   [Fic]   82-70403
ISBN 0-590-07828-3   AACR2

Published by Four Winds Press
A division of Scholastic Inc., New York, N.Y.
Copyright © 1982 by W. E. Butterworth
All rights reserved
Printed in the United States of America
Library of Congress Catalog Card Number: 82-70403
1 2 3 4 5 86 85 84 83 82

CHAPTER 1

TOM LOCKWOOD, WHO WAS FOURTEEN, BLOND, and tall for his age, turned the corner onto Palm Drive. He was on his ten-speed and riding no hands, not to show off but because there was no reason to ride bent over the handlebars. The road was flat and smooth, and there was very little traffic on it.

Boss and Bandit, the Lockwoods' Llewellin setters, were waiting for him. It might very well be a fact that canines cannot tell time, but it was also a fact that every school day at about three o'clock, Boss and Bandit stopped whatever they were doing and went to the corner of the fence, where they could expect to see Tom riding home from school.

There was a hurricane fence around most of the lot on which the Lockwood house was built. The only part of the lot that wasn't fenced was an area as wide as the house, between the house and the street. The fence, of heavy wire twisted into triangles, was eight feet tall and topped with barbed wire. It ran from one corner of the house out to the street, to the property line, then along the property line down the side of the lot to the rear, and then inside the bulkhead, which kept the backyard from sliding into the canal, back up the other property line, and then finally tied in with the other side of the house.

Every ten feet, at eye level, metal signs had been wired to the fence. Half of them had DANGER! HIGH VOLTAGE printed on them in red paint, with a lightning bolt, and the other half had WARNING! THIS PROPERTY PROTECTED BY K-9 DOGS!

1

The fence, and especially the signs, infuriated Grandmother Lockwood, who said it made the house look like a prison camp. Barbara, Tom's older sister, who was a newspaper reporter, thought the fence was funny, and when she wrote home, she addressed the letters to "Fort Lockwood."

There was no high voltage, and Bandit and Boss were lovable, if somewhat spoiled, Llewellins, not snarling and vicious K-9 dogs. Paul, Jr., Tom's seventeen-year-old brother, had found the signs in a storeroom at their father's plant and had carried them home. The plant was protected by K-9 dogs, and there were a dozen places at the plant where there was high voltage.

The fence was intended to keep in the dogs, who were littermates. The reason there were two of them was that Tom's father hadn't had the heart to leave Boss behind after he'd decided to buy Bandit.

Tom's mother had told him he was insane. Tom's father had replied that he had reached the age and position in life at which he could indulge his insanity, and now that that had been established, could they talk about something else?

Grandmother Lockwood didn't like to hear her son referred to as crazy, but she was willing to admit that Paul Lockwood, Sr., was a little eccentric. "Eccentricity," Grandmother Lockwood said, "is often a by-product of genius."

Tom wasn't sure that his father was a genius, but there was no question that he was eccentric and that he made a lot of money. He wasn't sure, either, what his father actually did. Sometimes Paul Lockwood, Sr., said he was a mathematician, and sometimes he said he was an electrical engineer. All Tom knew for certain was that his father worked with computers and that, just before he had been born, his father and Uncle Charley Walton had started a little company, as partners, in Uncle Charley's garage. The little company was now Wallwood Microtronics, Inc., with a plant a hundred miles away and, as the stationery said, "Offices in Principal Cities of the World."

2

Charley Walton, no uncle at all but a lifelong friend of the family, was Chairman of the Board and Chief Executive Officer, and Tom's father was Director of Research and Development. Tom's father had explained that one time: "I develop it," he said, "and Uncle Charley sells it." He did not explain what "it" was. Sometimes his father worked on it at the plant, and sometimes he went to Europe and Asia to work on it, but most of the time he worked on it in the nearby shop.

When the Lockwoods had built the house in Ocean Springs five years ago, the company had bought a lot three blocks away, inland, and on it had put up a house, which it had then turned into a combination office and workshop for Tom's father. The shop was off limits to just about everybody, including Tom's mother. Two Wallwood Microtronics employees—Mrs. Lopez, the "office manager," and her husband, whom Tom's father described as a self-taught electrical engineer—were the only people other than his father who had keys to the shop. Everybody else who wanted to go into the shop had to ring the bell.

Tom had been in the shop, of course. Inside it looked like a curious combination of office, TV repair shop, and classroom. Outside, in what should have been the living room, was Mrs. Lopez's office, which looked like a regular office, with a desk and telephones, an electric typewriter, and a Telex machine. Inside what would have been the bedrooms were workbenches loaded down with electronic equipment, desks and filing cabinets, and drafting tables. The walls of the smallest "bedroom" were covered with green chalkboards. The chalkboards were generally covered, either with mathematical formulas or with what Tom had learned to recognize as electronic schematic drawings.

The room with the chalkboards also had two computer keyboards. One was a terminal, connected to the big computer at the plant. The other was for the smaller computer Tom's father and Mr. Lopez had installed right there in the room for reasons Tom couldn't quite understand.

3

The shop was a five-minute walk down Palm Drive, the street the house was on, to Ocean Boulevard, and Tom's father either walked to work or drove in his Jeep, generally with Boss and Bandit beside him.

Most of the people in the neighborhood were businessmen or professional men. They went to work about the same time as Tom's father did. But they went to work in suits and ties, and Tom's father usually went to work in his hunting or fishing clothes, depending on the season.

That was the real reason, Tom's father said, that a group of citizens had gone to the City Council and protested that the shop was violating the zoning ordinances. It was a business, they said, and operating in a residential area was illegal.

"If I were they," his father said, "I'd hate me, too. Anybody who has to get dressed up in a shirt and tie and then spend from forty-five minutes to an hour in traffic getting to work has a right to hate somebody who doesn't."

The City Council heard the complaint and decided that his father was doing nothing that was illegal or that hurt the community. From the outside, the house looked like any other house. And no one was producing anything in the house, or selling anything, or making noise. Dr. Lockwood—the "Dr." was twice due Paul Lockwood, once for a Ph.D. in mathematics and again for a Ph.D. in electrical engineering—the City Council decided, was doing research, and research was not prohibited by the zoning ordinance as long as it didn't involve the use of guinea pigs, for example, or otherwise create a smell or some other disturbance.

Boss and Bandit, their tails wagging with delight, followed Tom down the fence to the gate and waited for him to open it and come through. They waited until he had rested the bike against the fence and laid his books on the grass. Then they rolled onto their backs, waved their paws in the air, and waited to have their chests scratched. It was the

4

same routine every day. They demanded that their chests be scratched a minimum of ninety seconds. There was no maximum; they never had too much of it. But they would permit him to stop after ninety seconds.

Tom had to scratch both chests simultaneously. If he scratched just Boss's chest, Bandit would whine. If he scratched just Bandit's chest, Boss would bare his teeth and growl menacingly at his brother until Bandit got the message and backed away. As far as Tom knew, Boss had never actually taken a bite at Bandit, but Bandit was convinced his threats were genuine.

When Tom tired of scratching their chests and pushed the bike up the driveway to the house, Boss and Bandit followed him, one on each side. The next step in the daily routine was the dog biscuit. Each dog was given a biscuit from a box kept in the garage. Bandit took his and ran with it to a far corner of the yard. Boss gulped his down on the spot and then ran after Bandit. Bandit ate his biscuit very slowly, holding it between his paws and taking tiny bites. Between bites, he growled at Boss to discourage any ideas Boss might have about helping himself to the dog biscuit. Still, despite this behavior, Tom was pretty sure Bandit had never bitten Boss to protect his biscuit, if only because Boss had never really tried to take it away from him.

Tom always waited patiently for Bandit to finish his dog biscuit so that he could take both dogs into the house with him. He had to, because the trouble with Boss and Bandit was that they were roamers. Whenever they grew bored with things in the yard, they took off. It was their nature, Tom's father said. A hunting dog could logically be expected to hunt. And to them the fence was nothing more than a minor inconvenience.

"You may understand their roaming instinct," Tom's mother had told his father before the fence was built, "but our neighbors don't. And they don't like our dogs in their

5

backyards. Boss and Bandit have chased Mrs. Cortell's poor little cat right through her rose arbor. You're going to have to do something about it."

"Like what?"

"Like get them a pen or something. Or fence in part of the backyard."

Tom's father investigated pens, taking Tom with him to the kennels of the man who had taught him how to train the dogs. The kennels there, called runs, were like cages.

"That won't do at all," his father reported on the way home. "Boss and Bandit are sensitive, highly intelligent animals. It would cause them irreparable psychological damage to be jailed like that."

Tom's father believed that when you didn't know much about what you were doing, you should find someone who did. He decided the expert he needed was Colonel Switzer, the plant engineer. Colonel Switzer was a retired army officer who had served thirty years in the corps of engineers before coming to work for Wallwood Microtronics. A retired army engineer, Dr. Lockwood said, should know what it was necessary to know about fences.

"It's going to have to be a taller fence than the one around the shop," Paul Lockwood told Colonel Switzer. "They can jump right over that one."

"No problem," Colonel Switzer announced.

Dr. Lockwood also told Colonel Switzer that he wanted the fence built as quickly as possible. The neighbors seemed on the point of revolution.

"The boys and I are going quail hunting in Georgia over the Thanksgiving holiday," he said. "And my wife is going to see our daughter. See if you can get a fence put up while we're all gone. Enclose as much of the yard as possible."

"No problem," Colonel Switzer repeated.

It turned out the colonel knew all about fences but not too much about dogs or architectural beauty. While the Lockwoods were away for the Thanksgiving holiday, a crew from the plant arrived at the house and built the eight-foot fence, topped with angled mounts holding three strands of barbed wire.

That was when 124 Palm Drive had become Fort Lockwood.

Some of the neighbors had been nearly as furious as Tom's mother when they saw it. They were convinced Dr. Lockwood had put up the fence for spite. The residents of Palm Drive took great pride in the wide, luxuriant lawns that, altogether, stretched from one end of the street to the other. And now the unbroken expanse of green was cut by eight feet of hurricane fence and eighteen inches of barbed wire, suspended between sturdy galvanized steel poles set in concrete.

Mrs. Lockwood said that it simply would have to come down.

Dr. Lockwood said that, for one thing, the company had sent him a large bill for the fence, and he had no intention of throwing away that kind of money. For another, Colonel Switzer had gone out of his way to design the fence and to arrange for the crew to put it up on Thanksgiving Day, and he had no intention of hurting the colonel's feelings by having it torn down. And, finally, she had asked for a fence to keep the dogs in, and he'd provided one.

The fence stayed, but it did not do what it was intended to do. Boss and Bandit took one look at their brand-new galvanized wire prison, sniffed at it, looked up at the barbed wire eight feet over them, and immediately wiggled their way under the bottom of the fence, which was four inches off the lawn.

Fifteen minutes after Boss and Bandit were first "locked up," Mrs. Cortell was on the telephone, icily demanding that someone come immediately and rescue her Oscar from the roof of her garage, onto which Oscar had been chased by those "vicious brutes."

"Improper planning," Dr. Lockwood said. "But no

problem. I see the fix. Paul and Tom can do it in an afternoon, after school."

The problem, as Tom's father saw it, was that the fence, between its posts, was flexible. Boss and Bandit had been able to escape simply by pushing it out of the way in the middle. The solution was a band of galvanized steel that would be woven through the bottom of the fence and fastened securely to the poles.

It took Paul and Tom considerably more than one afternoon to do the work. For one thing, Boss and Bandit concluded that since Paul and Tom were on their hands and knees in the backyard, they wanted to play. It is difficult and time-consuming to weave galvanized-steel strips through the bottom of a fence while you are on your knees and two Llewellin setters are licking your face and neck and nibbling your ears. For another thing, there was much more fence to weave the galvanized-steel strips through than anyone had realized.

But finally the fence, Mark II, was finished. Tom's father examined what they had done and gave his approval. The bottom of the hurricane fence was now just about as stiff as it could be.

"First class," Tom's father said. "I'd like to see them get through that fence now."

They went into the house to get a celebration can of beer for Paul Lockwood, Sr., and Paul Lockwood, Jr., and a can of 7-Up for Tom Lockwood. When they went back to the yard to reexamine the fruits of their labor, Boss and Bandit had already dug under it and were off to pay their respects to Mrs. Cortell and her cat.

That was why Tom Lockwood had to take the dogs into the house whenever possible.

Another part of Boss and Bandit's routine was going hunting with the male Lockwoods. Usually they did this on a Friday, which meant that it was a school day.

As Tom and Paul Lockwood saw it, one of their father's more interesting eccentricities was that he was not at all concerned with their earning a perfect attendance record at school. Quite the contrary. He believed that taking a day off now and then "flushed the mind" and made it more receptive to the acquisition and retention of knowledge. The school authorities were generally furnished with a letter saying that Tom and Paul had been absent because they had had the opportunity to go on a "field trip."

"If I said I was taking you hunting," Tom's father said, "they would form a mental picture of us crashing wild-eyed through the woods, slaughtering innocent wildlife."

It wasn't that way at all, Tom thought. It was more like they were taking an excursion into Boss and Bandit's lives. They had taken the dogs into theirs, teaching them manners and how to give their paws and housebreaking them, and now the dogs were showing them how things were in nature.

As soon as they reached the fields, Boss and Bandit would whine for permission to hunt, and as soon as it was given, they would start to search the fields with their noses, sweeping back and forth until they picked up the scent of quail. Then they would follow the scent until they came upon a covey or a single bird.

At that point, the "vicious brutes" who ran Mrs. Cortell's Oscar up on her garage roof would become just as graceful and skilled as a ballet dancer. With every muscle as stiff as wire, they would move very, very slowly toward the quail, in absolute silence, taking sometimes thirty seconds to lower a paw to the ground and then thirty seconds to put the other paw down.

Finally, they would tuck one paw up under their chest, stick their tails out horizontally behind them, and freeze. This was the "point." The spot at which their noses pointed was the quails' hiding place. They would hold the point until the Lockwoods walked up on them and flushed the birds.

9

No matter which of the dogs first picked up a scent, Boss always "made the point" before Bandit. Bandit never got in front of him. He took up his point five yards or a little more behind Boss. He "honored" Boss's point.

But after the birds had been flushed and had soared with flapping wings into the air, then, if one had fallen before the humans' shotguns, it was Bandit's turn. He would race ahead of Boss to where the bird lay, snatch it in his mouth, and, with a proud walk like a trained horse in a circus, carry it to the humans and drop it at their feet.

"The cooperation of man and beast," Tom's father would say. "One of the most beautiful sights in nature."

They always ate what they shot.

Tom's father had once "behaved very badly," as his mother put it, when she had entertained people from the university with broiled quail. (Mrs. Lockwood was a teacher there and a candidate for a Ph.D. in music.) One of Mrs. Lockwood's fellow teachers had held out his hands in front of him, rejecting the quail with the announcement that he just didn't have the heart to eat something that had been killed by hunters.

Tom's father, who always seemed to drink more than usual when Mrs. Lockwood's friends were coming to dinner, had looked at him in disbelief. Then he had said, "No problem. What we'll do is send somebody out to the egg farm and get you a chicken that died of old age."

Tom knew there was something his father did when he was hunting or fishing that he didn't talk about. He thought. By looking at his father's face when they were in the field or on the boat, Tom could tell whether he was thinking about hunting or fishing, or about some problem he was having at the shop. When he was thinking about his work, he would wrinkle his eyebrows and sometimes his mouth and occasionally he would take a notebook from his pocket and write.

When they were in the field one day not long after Boss

and Bandit had dug their way under the fence, Paul Lockwood did all of the above. But it wasn't his work he was thinking about; it was what to do about the dogs.

"Psychological warfare!" he announced triumphantly, just before they quit for the day. "We'll psych the beasties."

C H A P T E R 2

WHEN TOM GOT HOME FROM SCHOOL THE next Monday, the van with Wallwood Microtronic's logo was in the driveway, and the first thing Tom thought was that something was wrong with the television again. Tom's father believed it was foolish to have a TV repairman work on their television sets when there was not only "a fortune" in test equipment in the shop, but himself and Mr. Lopez as well. A television set, he pointed out, as complicated as it might appear to the layman, was really a very simple device compared to the microelectronics with which he and Mr. Lopez worked every day. Sometimes the Lockwoods went without one of their TVs for a week when Tom's father and Mr. Lopez ran into "unexpected problems" while fixing it.

But there was nothing wrong with the television. Tom's father and Mr. Lopez were in the backyard, preparing to wage psychological warfare on—to "psych-out"—Boss and Bandit.

"Don't go out there, Tom," Mrs. Lockwood said. "You know your father doesn't like to be disturbed when he's working. And when Paul comes home, you tell him what I said."

Paul was a senior in high school and got home half an hour after Tom got home from the junior high. Or sometimes later, now that he had his driver's license and had discovered girls.

Tom looked out the dining-room window and saw Mr. Lopez and his father hard at work on something they had set

12

up near the fence. Whatever it was had a loudspeaker attached to it. Aside from that, Tom couldn't tell anything about it.

Tom played with Boss and Bandit until Paul came home. Then both boys looked out the dining-room window and tried to guess what their father and Mr. Lopez were up to.

At a quarter to six, looking smug, Mr. Lopez and Dr. Lockwood came into the kitchen. They made themselves a drink and Dr. Lockwood sent Tom to fetch his mother, so that she could witness how he and Mr. Lopez had settled the dog and fence problem once and for all, utilizing the amazing capabilities of electronics.

"What it is," Tom's father said, "is a rather simple application of the intruder detection device, or burglar alarm."

"Paul," Mrs. Lockwood said, "the dogs are getting out, not sneaking in."

Her husband gave her a pained look and ordered Boss and Bandit turned loose in the backyard. Everybody went outside and watched from the patio. Boss and Bandit went nowhere near the fence. Boss went to the device Tom's father and Mr. Lopez had built, sniffed it suspiciously, and then raised his leg. Dr. Lockwood had told Tom that was the way canines marked the territory they considered their own.

Mrs. Lockwood giggled.

"They know better than to try to get under the fence when we're out here watching them," his father said. "Everybody into the house."

They all went to the dining room and gathered around the window. The dogs were lying down and showed no inclination at all to go near the fence.

"They must sense we're watching them," Dr. Lockwood said finally. "So everybody away from the window."

"What is that thing, anyway?" Tom asked. "A dog stereo?"

"A stereo," Dr. Lockwood said icily, "has two or more speakers. There's only one speaker out there."

"What's it for, Pop?" Paul, Jr., pursued.

"You'll see soon enough," Dr. Lockwood said significantly. He looked at his wife. "When do we eat?"

Tom had just split his baked potato and was putting butter into the cavity when there came a crash of cymbals and a voice, his father's, bellowing "Bad Dog! Bad Dog! Bad Dog!" over and over again.

His mother was cringing. His father wore a look of self-satisfaction. Everybody ran to the dining-room window.

"What it does," Dr. Lockwood explained, "is detect, by induction, anything—the dogs, in this case—approaching the fence. The circuit triggers a relay, which activates a tape recording of my voice. Plus, of course, that cymbal sound. I took that from the *1812 Overture.*"

Darkness had fallen, and they couldn't see anything in the backyard. Tom ran into the kitchen and flicked on the lights.

Boss was holding a perfect point, as if the loudspeaker booming Dr. Lockwood's voice were a covey of quail. Bandit was three-quarters of the way under the fence and, as they watched, squirmed the rest of his body through, gained his feet, and took off as fast as he could in the direction of Mrs. Cortell's cat.

"Well, it stopped at least one of them," Tom's father said.

But when the sensor no longer detected Bandit's body touching the fence, it sent the appropriate signal, and the tape recording of Dr. Lockwood's voice shut off. Boss held his point another thirty seconds, then dropped it. He looked over his shoulder at the house, advanced on the loudspeaker, lifted his leg again, and then followed Bandit's route under the fence.

"Pop," Paul, Jr., said, "if you'd only let me know you

14

were going to arrange all this, I could've sold enough tickets to pay for the fence."

Paul Lockwood looked at his son with his eyebrows raised as far as his skin would allow. Then he laughed. "This is what happens when you underestimate the opposition," he said.

If he had said something like that, Tom thought, he would have been boiled in oil, had his head cut off, or at the very least heard his mother shriek, "Don't you dare mock your father." He wondered if Paul got away with that sort of thing because he was older, or just because he was his father's clone. He looked like his father, he thought like his father, and he had already been accepted by M.I.T., not because his father had gone there but because of the scores he'd gotten on a special test they gave students who had "demonstrated unusual mathematical aptitude."

Tom had unusual mathematical aptitude himself. He was right on the edge of flunking algebra. The only thing funny about that was that when his parents had gone to the school for a conference with his algebra teacher, Miss Conyers had asked his father if he happened to know someone with training in mathematics who could tutor Tom. She had flashed an understanding smile and told him it had been her "experience that most parents remembered very little of their junior-high-school mathematics."

Before his mother could open her mouth, Tom's father had replied, "My wife has a college education, Miss Conyers, and she has a splendid memory. I'm sure she'll be able to help Tom."

Tom's mother remembered about as much algebra as Tom had learned. Paul had been his reluctant tutor.

"Are you really this stupid, or are you putting me on?" Paul had asked, more than once, when Tom hadn't been able to remember the necessary steps to solve a problem.

It could all be genetics, Tom thought. Paul had inherited mathematical genes from their father, and he hadn't. The trouble with that theory was that if children didn't inherit the genes of one parent, they were supposed to inherit those of the other. He should, in other words, be musical, as his mother was. But he had about as much musical talent as he had mathematical. The only conclusion to be drawn was that by the time his parents had gotten around to having him, the supply of smart genes was all gone, soaked up like a blotter by his older sister and brother.

The next exercise in dog control was a steel cable strung tightly between two poles. Boss and Bandit were hooked to the cable by lengths of thin chain. It took them about twenty minutes to wrap themselves up in it until they couldn't move. Two more poles and another piece of cable were erected, at a precisely measured distance far enough away from the first set of poles and cable to keep them from getting tangled up.

From the moment they were born, Boss and Bandit had been close to each other. They simply couldn't understand why they were now being separated and couldn't sleep curled up together or eat from the same bowl, as they always had.

"It isn't the howling that gets to me," Dr. Lockwood said, "it's that hurt look in their eyes."

Paul put the poles and cable nearest the house to work as an antenna for his short-wave radio receiver. The other poles and cable just sat in the backyard. When Uncle Charley came to visit and saw them, he said that if they had used a stronger piece of cable, they could have rented them to the circus for the high-wire walkers to practice on.

"If you're so smart, Charley," Tom's mother said, "you tell us what to do about those dogs."

"All you have to do, Caroline," Uncle Charley said, "is extend the fence into the ground. Give me a piece of paper and I'll show you what I mean."

He sketched what he saw as a simple, foolproof solution to the dogs getting under the fence. First a ditch would be

16

dug, two feet deep and eighteen inches or so wide. Then a strip of woven fencing material would be fastened to the bottom of the existing fence, with its bottom laid flat in the hole. Then the dirt would be put back in the hole and the grass replaced.

"That way, you see, when they try to dig under the fence, they'll come up against the fence laid flat in the ground. That'll stop them."

Tom had visions of himself spending the next several months after school digging a ditch two feet deep and eighteen inches wide around the whole fence.

While he was there they took Uncle Charley quail hunting with them, and Boss and Bandit seemed to sense that they were being shown off. Their performance in the field was perfect.

"I suppose, when you've got a matched pair like those two," Uncle Charley said, "you have to expect to pay for it. You don't want to lose those dogs, Paul, no matter what it costs to keep them inside the fence."

Tom and Paul didn't have to dig the trench for the fence. A short, fat man with a flowing mustache showed up at the house and unloaded a baby bulldozer from a trailer. He handed Mrs. Lockwood a business card that identified him as Carlos Santiago, Landscaping Contractor, Septic Tanks, Drainage Fields, and Driveways Built.

Mr. Santiago didn't speak much English, and Mrs. Lockwood did not speak Spanish. Mr. Lopez was summoned from the shop. Mr. Lopez showed Mr. Santiago what services he was expected to perform. Mr. Lopez had a hard time explaining to Mr. Santiago that all that was required was a ditch two feet deep and eighteen inches wide all around the inside of the fence, but finally Mr. Santiago went to work, leaving no doubt whatsoever that he thought the Lockwood family deserved to be inside an eight-foot-tall hurricane fence topped with three strands of barbed wire.

Mr. Santiago's baby bulldozer was heavier than it

looked. It tore up the lawn on the way back and forth to the fence and made the area around the trench it dug look "like a battlefield," according to Grandmother Lockwood. "All you need to complete it," she said, "is a flag and some sandbags."

Attaching the extra piece of fence to the existing fence wasn't nearly as hard as Tom thought it would be. The hard work came in shoveling the dirt back in the trench on top of the fence. Mrs. Lockwood announced that if Mr. Santiago drove his baby bulldozer across her lawn again, he would do so over her dead body.

For some reason, it seemed that there was more dirt to put back in the trench than had been taken out, for when Tom and Paul were finished, there was an eight-inch mound of raw earth where the trench had been. Grandmother Lockwood said it now looked like "the world's longest grave."

"A simple problem of compaction," Dr. Lockwood announced. They all climbed into the Jeep and went to an equipment rental store, where they rented a roller. The roller was a steel drum with a handle on it, like that on a wagon. They lifted it up and placed it carefully in the back of the Jeep. Tom wondered how dragging a steel drum on top of the ditch, which he now thought of as "the grave," was going to help anything.

When they got to the house, he found out. Dr. Lockwood got out the hose and filled the drum with water. Then the roller sank even deeper into the lawn than Mr. Santiago's baby bulldozer had sunk, and they had to pump out about half of the water before it was light enough for all three of them to drag across the yard to the grave.

Once there, however, it performed as Dr. Lockwood had said it would. The mound was compacted. It was still not quite level with the rest of the lawn, but it would settle in time, Dr. Lockwood said, and you'd never know that a ditch had been dug. The raw earth was sprinkled with a quick-growing grass seed that would hold it in place until the Bermuda grass of the rest of the lawn could grow over it.

Bandit and Boss, who had been confined to the house during the trench digging and taken for walks on leashes, were turned loose in the backyard. They started at one end of the fence and moved to the other with their noses to the freshly seeded earth. And then Bandit started to dig.

Dr. Lockwood's face beamed.

"Wait till he hits the buried fence," he said. "He will then know defeat."

It took Bandit about a minute of frenzied digging, during which a steady stream of freshly seeded dirt sprayed from his paws over the lawn, until he hit the woven steel wire of the sunken fence. He stopped his furious digging and put one paw rather delicately into the hole, cocking his head to show his confusion. Then he put his nose all the way into the hole and sniffed. Boss's curiosity was aroused, and he walked over to the hole.

"Bandit's getting a second opinion," Dr. Lockwood said. "But it won't do him a bit of good."

Boss sniffed the hole, made a couple of tentative stabs with his paw, and then walked away. Bandit walked after him. Then they curled up together and went to sleep.

Two hours later, Mrs. Cortell telephoned to announce that this time it was only by the grace of God that poor Oscar had been spared. If Dr. Lockwood didn't make *some* effort to control his vicious animals, she would have to speak to her lawyer.

"I think it would be a lot cheaper to buy her dumb cat and feed it to them," Tom said.

"Tom!" Mrs. Lockwood gasped. "What an absolutely rotten thing to even think, much less say! You ought to be ashamed of yourself!"

"If they wanted to hurt Oscar," Dr. Lockwood said, "they would have done it a long time ago. They just like to chase him, that's all."

"I wonder how they got out," Tom said.

"I'm almost afraid to find out," Dr. Lockwood replied.

19

When they retrieved the dogs at Mrs. Cortell's house, they saw that the dogs' normally soft and fluffy fur was matted and stained with dirt. Boss and Bandit had obviously dug under the fence again. But where? When they got home and examined the fence, they saw what had happened. The hole Bandit had originally dug was now about five feet long. Either Bandit or Boss had returned to the hole and continued to dig it until he reached the end of the buried section of fence, and had then dug under the fence.

But this time the dogs' escape was not entirely funny. When the Lockwoods stood them under a hose in the backyard to wash the mud out of their coats, they found blood mixed with the dirt. Both animals had torn their skin and paws badly on the cut ends of the fence while digging under it to make their escape.

It was necessary to take them to the veterinarian for treatment, and, in Boss's case, to suture a really nasty cut in one of the pads of his left front foot. The paw had to be bandaged, and for the next ten days it required constant attention, including muzzling Boss at night to keep him from tearing the bandage off his paw.

That marked the end of what Grandmother Lockwood called "the great jailbreak caper." Except when there was someone to watch them in the backyard, Boss and Bandit were confined to the house. Their instinct to roam could not be controlled, so they simply could not be left alone. Dogs, Dr. Lockwood said, unfortunately did not have "a constitutional guarantee of life, liberty, and the pursuit of cats."

"Anyway," he added, "they can still chase the boat."

Mrs. Lockwood did not think that boat chasing was any funnier than cat chasing. But Dr. Lockwood considered it one of the bright spots in his life.

Across the canal from the houses on Palm Drive was a remote corner of the municipal beach, a spit of land between the canal and the Gulf of Mexico. Grandmother Lockwood referred to it as "Lover's Lane by the Sea," because it was used entirely by young people who seemed far more interested in each other, and in their suntans, than in the waters of the Gulf.

Dr. Lockwood was unable to understand sunbathers. "The evidence is in," he said. "People who bake themselves in the sun are inviting, at the very least, wrinkled and leathery skin before they're thirty and, at worst, skin cancer."

"The girls go there to meet boys, Paul," Mrs. Lockwood defended them.

"Girls can meet all the boys they want in the shade," he said. "You never let Barbara do that, and you never did it in the olden days."

"Barbara got all the tan she wanted on the boat," Mrs. Lockwood said.

"Be that as it may, neither you nor she ever baked your brains out on the beach," he said. "The dogs are providing a humanitarian service, saving those idiots from falling asleep in the sun and really hurting themselves."

What the dogs did, whenever they were not taken out in the boat with Dr. Lockwood and Paul and Tom, was leap into the canal, swim across it, and then race along the beach, yelping, in pursuit of the boat as it made its way down the canal and then through the inlet and out into the Gulf. They regarded the sunbathers as nothing more than minor obstacles in their path, to be jumped over or run across, or, sometimes, if luck was with them, as sources of hot dogs, hamburgers, and ice cream, which were obligingly left in positions from which they could be grabbed by dogs on the run. The voyage of the good ship *GIGO* to the Gulf was often accompanied by the roars of outraged sunbathers.

CHAPTER 3

PAUL LOCKWOOD, JR., GRADUATED FROM HIGH school that June. He was the valedictorian. He was awarded the Wachtell Prize ($500) for excellence in mathematics, an academic scholarship to M.I.T., a Japanese watch containing two circuit chips that did everything but make breakfast, and the biggest prize of all: an invitation to work in the shop with his father and Mr. Lopez during the summer.

All of this, of course, reminded Tom that he had been at the end of the line when brains were being passed out, and that they were all gone by the time he'd gotten to the head of the line. He was going to have to spend two hours every morning in summer school, having failed to pass his final algebra examination by two points. Passing was 70, and he had made 68.

"What this means, you understand," Tom's brother pointed out to him, "is that you have effectively screwed up any vacation the family might have gone on. You have to be in summer school, and anybody who has to use his fingers and toes to count over ten obviously cannot be left home alone."

Tom told himself that the only reason he had not punched his brother in the mouth was because calm logic had prevailed. Paul was still larger than he was. Though that situation was obviously changing. Next year, if he continued his present rate of growth, he would be as large as Paul. He could punch him then. The opportunity would certainly present itself.

22

Discretion proved to be its own reward. Paul's exalted status as an apprentice in the shop lasted one day—until their father learned of a large hole in Paul's education.

It came out at dinner.

"Are you aware that the valedictorian here can't type?" Dr. Lockwood inquired of his wife.

"What do you mean?" she asked.

"Type. Operate a typewriter," Dr. Lockwood said.

"Yes, I suppose I am," she said.

"And you did nothing about it?" Dr. Lockwood asked incredulously.

"Like what?"

"You don't seem very concerned," Dr. Lockwood accused.

"Guilty," she said. "I shamefully confess my failure as a mother. What's the difference?"

"You astonish me," Dr. Lockwood said. "You really astonish me. The difference is, for one thing, that I can't use him in the shop."

"I don't know what you're talking about," Mrs. Lockwood said.

"Typing is as essential a tool in our technological society as is the ability to drive an automobile," Dr. Lockwood said. "I don't see how they can hand anyone who can't type a high-school diploma."

"They don't teach typing in the college prep courses," Mrs. Lockwood replied. "That's why he can't type."

"You're kidding," Dr. Lockwood said.

"I am not."

"I can type," Tom offered.

"You can type?" his father asked.

"Yes, sir."

"How is it that you can type and your brother can't?"

"I did it for Boy Scouts," Tom replied.

"For *Boy Scouts?*"

"Yes, sir. For the typing merit badge," Tom replied.

"Obviously," Dr. Lockwood said, "the Boy Scouts have a much clearer view of the real world than the morons who established the curricula at the high school."

"Just because you disagree with them, Paul," Mrs. Lockwood said, "doesn't make them morons."

Dr. Lockwood snorted.

"We'll have to find a fix," he said. "In the meantime, Tom can come to work in the shop in the afternoons, after summer school. He'll have to—I've been counting on some help."

"And what am I going to be doing?" Paul, Jr., asked.

"You're going to learn how to type," Dr. Lockwood replied. "By the time you go to Cambridge in September, you will be an accomplished typist."

"Why?" Paul asked. "And why can't I help in the shop?"

"You haven't been listening," Dr. Lockwood said. "Because typing is an essential skill. You have noticed, I hope, the typewriter-type keyboards in front of the computer terminals?"

"Sure."

"*Ergo sum,*" his father said.

"What's that mean?" Paul, Jr., asked.

"The facts speak for themselves," Tom said.

"How do *you* know?" Paul, Jr., demanded.

"Pop says it all the time," Tom said. "I looked it up."

"What was the name of that guy on the board of education who grabbed me at the graduation and told me he would be 'grateful for my input'?" Dr. Lockwood asked.

"Dr. Jernigan," Mrs. Lockwood replied. "What about him?"

"I've got a good mind to call him up and give him the input that he ought to be ashamed of himself for turning out high-school graduates who can't type," Dr. Lockwood said. "It's outrageous. It's almost criminal."

"You will not," Mrs. Lockwood said firmly.

"He asked for it," Dr. Lockwood said.

"That isn't the kind of input he had in mind," Mrs. Lockwood replied. "He was talking about the math curricula."

"A mathematician who can't type is as handicapped as a one-armed paper hanger," Dr. Lockwood said. "But don't worry, I won't tell him. I'm not sure he'd understand."

While Tom was off at the high school, where all summer school sessions were held, taking Algebra I again, Paul stayed home and tried to teach himself how to type. In the afternoon, they both went to the shop. Mrs. Lopez taught Tom how to use the Telex machine and the word processor, and Paul wielded a broom and otherwise made himself useful.

It wasn't a complete victory for Tom, for operating the word processor was very difficult. Tom understood literally nothing of what he was typing. It was most often two or three lines of explanatory text (which he didn't understand) and then a page, or pages, of mathematical formulas and equations. It had to be absolutely perfect, and despite what his father had said about mathematicians typing, what Tom worked from was either his father's or Mr. Lopez's written notes, or, worse, what they had scrawled on one of the chalkboards. When he had to take the information from the chalkboard, he had to copy it onto a sheet of paper and then type from his own notes.

If it hadn't been for Paul's pushing a broom while he sat in front of the word processor, Tom would have hated it. Whenever he sensed Paul looking at him, Tom would give him a warm smile of brotherly love and understanding. That generally served to get Paul pushing the broom again. And it gave Tom a feeling of real satisfaction.

The work schedule wasn't rigid. Sometimes, when Tom and Paul went to the shop after lunch, neither their father nor Mr. Lopez was there, and there was nothing much for them to do. Other times, "the guys in the plant"—in other words, the engineers and technicians at the other end of the tie-lines that connected the shop's computer, Telex, and word processor with the plant—ran into some kind of difficulty, and the lights in the shop burned late at night. But there was generally time every day to water-ski or drag for shrimp, and most weekends they got up early so they could be twenty miles off shore, at the hundred-fathom curve, when the sun came up and fishing was supposed to be at its best.

It was usually just the three of them. Mrs. Lockwood wasn't much of a fisherman, and Mr. Lopez frankly admitted hating the water. Boss and Bandit, however, generally went along in the *GIGO*.

GIGO was a term from the shop. People who worked with computers were always saying that if you fed bad data (garbage) to a computer, you were sure to get useless data (garbage) back. Hence, Garbage In, Garbage Out, or GIGO.

Barbara came home for one week of her two-weeks' vacation, bringing with her a reporter from her newspaper whom she insisted was just a "good friend." It was something of a disaster, because her good friend, who was about six foot three and looked as if he could have played pro football, hadn't ever been deep-sea fishing before.

With a massive display of willpower, he kept himself from being seasick all the way out to the hundred-fathom curve. The minute they slowed the *GIGO* down to trolling speed, however, the side-to-side rocking motion became too much for him, and he got sick. Bandit thought the big man leaning over the railing making those strange noises wanted to play, and he rested his paws on the railing beside him and barked at him. Boss, more suspicious, took up a perfect point.

"He felt humiliated enough," Barbara complained bitterly to her mother when they had finally returned to land, "without your husband and your sons having hysterics. I've never been so embarrassed in my life."

Dr. Lockwood made a valiant effort to make up for it that night by taking everybody out to a restaurant he ordinarily condemned for its small portions and high prices. But that was the last anybody ever saw of Barbara's "good friend."

The weekend that summer school was over (Tom passed Algebra I with an 87), Uncle Charley came down with his twin daughters, Anne and Marie, who were a year younger than Tom. "This is purely a business trip, of course," he said. "But while we're here, we might as well check out the rumor that the king are running."

With all those people going, there was no room for Boss and Bandit, and rather elaborate plans were made to leave them behind. The dogs knew that a fishing trip was in the offing, because they saw Tom and Paul loading the ice chests and the tackle aboard. They seemed surprised when, instead of heading for the boat first thing in the morning, the humans instead sat down and had a leisurely breakfast.

They weren't going out to the hundred-fathom curve. Dr. Lockwood had talked on the ship-to-ship with one of the charter boat captains who was a friend of his and had learned from him that the king mackerel were running, but close to shore, no more than a mile off the beach. They would start to feed about eight-thirty or nine o'clock, so there was no need to get up in the middle of the night. The Lockwoods could reach their fishing grounds twenty minutes after they got into the *GIGO*.

After breakfast, Boss and Bandit were enticed upstairs with pieces of toast and locked in Tom's room. Then everybody except Mrs. Lockwood ran out the back door and got into the *GIGO*. They could hear Boss and Bandit barking.

They'd been moving down the canal about three minutes when Tom saw the dogs at the fence. "They're out," he said.

"Your mother probably let them get away from her

27

town, for Oscar had been lying on the porch, giving himself a bath.

When Boss and Bandit didn't show up for supper, concern grew. Paul, Jr., got into the Jeep and went looking for them, and Tom and his father got into the boat and went through the inlet and up and down the Gulf beaches to see if they had found another cat to chase, or some other dogs to romp with.

Boss and Bandit could not be found.

Mrs. Lockwood said it was probably nothing to worry about, that they might very well be in pursuit of a female in season. Male dogs, she reminded them, were known to travel miles and stay away from home for days when they were after a female.

As soon as the Waltons had left for home the next morning, the Lockwoods went looking for Boss and Bandit again, driving slowly up and down the streets in both the Jeep and the station wagon, continually blowing two sharp blasts on whistles. Since they were twelve-week-old pups, Boss and Bandit had never ignored the signal to "come."

That afternoon they called the dog pound and then, fearfully, the police, to ask if there had been a report of dogs being run over. Neither the dog warden nor the police had had any word on a matched set of Llewellin setters.

The police sergeant on duty made the mistake of telling Dr. Lockwood that the police had better things to do with their time than look for a couple of dogs. Dr. Lockwood called the mayor and reminded him that when he and Mr. Lopez had, as a public service and without charge, gotten the new police radio system to work after all the technicians in town had not been able to, the mayor had told him that anytime he could be of service, Dr. Lockwood should not hesitate to call.

Ten minutes later, on Paul, Jr.'s police band radio, they heard the order for all cars to keep an eye out for either a matched pair of Llewellin setters or a pack of dogs romancing a lady dog. It was no joke, the police radio operator said—the order had come from the mayor himself.

The chief of police came to the house the next day to tell them that the police had found half a dozen lady dogs in season, but that there had been no Llewellin setters among their suitors.

"Well, they didn't just vanish from the face of the earth," Dr. Lockwood said. "They have to be somewhere."

"I wanted to talk to you about that, Paul," the chief of police said. "Yours aren't the only dogs we've lost around here in the last couple of months."

"You're leading up to something."

"What our experience has been, Paul, I'm sorry to tell you," the chief said, "is that if the dog warden doesn't catch them, or if they don't come back by themselves, we just don't get them back."

"What happens to them?"

"There's a market for dogs," the chief said.

"You think somebody stole them?"

"It's a distinct possibility," the chief said.

"What good would they be to somebody else?" Tom asked. He saw by the uncomfortable look on the chief's face that he had asked a question the chief didn't want to answer.

"You ever see a better pair of bird dogs?" Paul, Jr., asked sarcastically. "Dogs like that are worth a lot of money."

"What sportsman would buy dogs unless he knew where they came from?" Dr. Lockwood asked.

"He's not talking about that," Tom said. "Are you, Mr. Fogel?"

"Well, certainly, we have to consider that possibility," the chief said.

"What else, then?" Paul, Jr., asked, as much of Tom as of the chief of police.

"For a laboratory, you mean?" Dr. Lockwood asked.

"Yes," the chief said. "That, too."

"Littermates would be valuable in a laboratory," Dr. Lockwood said. "For purposes of comparison." He had trouble controlling his voice.

"You mean somebody stole Boss and Bandit to sell them to somebody who's going to experiment on them?" Paul, Jr., said.

"We don't know that, Paul," Dr. Lockwood said.

"I'd just like to catch somebody doing that!" Paul, Jr., said. His voice sounded strange, as if he were on the verge of tears.

"So would we, Paul," Chief Fogel said softly.

"Is that what you think, chief?" Dr. Lockwood asked.

"Paul," the chief said gently, "when something like this happens, the best thing to do is get another dog. That takes some of the pain away."

"Another dog? After Boss and Bandit?" Paul said. "Never!"

Then he couldn't stop himself and started to cry. Dr. Lockwood put his arms around him.

CHAPTER 4

THE LOCKWOODS DIDN'T GIVE UP ON BOSS and Bandit right away, of course. They did everything they could think of to get them back. They ran off fifty copies of a sign—LOST DOGS $200 REWARD—eleven by fourteen inches, as large as the shop's copier could make, and tacked them up all over town. They put a classified ad in the newspaper, and then, when they got no response, a two-inch ad in the news section. Dr. Lockwood even bought "spots" on the radio station. Nothing helped.

"It's as if they *did* vanish from the face of the earth," Dr. Lockwood said.

"If I were sure that's what happened, I'd feel a lot better," Tom replied.

"We're not going to talk about that," Dr. Lockwood said. "We're not even going to think about it."

Even Barbara got into the act. She was friendly with the chief editorial writer of the newspaper she worked for, the largest in the state, and she wrote a thunderous editorial condemning dognappers and urging the legislature to pass a law "with teeth in it."

Three weeks after Boss and Bandit disappeared, Dr. Lockwood came into breakfast and told Paul, Jr., that if he had any manners, he would wait to eat until his guest came to the table.

"What guest?" Paul, Jr., asked, baffled.

"The one who left his wheels blocking the driveway," Dr. Lockwood replied.

"What wheels?" Paul, Jr., asked. He and Tom got up from the table and opened the kitchen door. There was a car in the driveway: a shiny, yellow, three-year-old Triumph convertible. Paul, Jr.'s curiosity was now fully aroused, for he devoutly believed that Triumph automobiles generally, and yellow Triumph convertibles specifically, were the ultimate in automotive beauty.

"Whoever owns it," Paul, Jr., announced, "doesn't appreciate what he's got. He left the top down overnight. He'll have condensation all over the inside."

He went and examined the car more closely.

"You don't know who that belongs to?" Dr. Lockwood asked.

"Haven't the faintest," Paul, Jr., said. "I'd *know* if any friend of mine had a set of wheels like that."

"See if the registration's in the glove compartment," Dr. Lockwood suggested.

Paul, Jr., opened the glove compartment and found the registration. After looking at it, he seemed stunned.

"Let me see," Tom said, and snatched it from his fingers.

"Hey, Pop!" Paul, Jr., said.

"I don't believe it," Tom said.

"Don't expect anything else for Christmas or your birthday or any other occasion for the next twenty years," Dr. Lockwood said. "And you may consider it the carrot dangling before the jackass's nose. It will miraculously disappear the first time your grade-point average drops below three point zero."

The Triumph helped a little to get Boss and Bandit out of their minds, but it wasn't a complete cure. Tom realized, too, that the only reason his mother had stood for his father's buying Paul, Jr., the car was that the object was to cheer him up. The proof of that came when Dr. Lockwood asked Tom if there was something he had his heart set on. After all, he didn't want Tom to feel like the family orphan.

34

"Let me have an IOU," Tom replied. "I need time to think of something useless that I want."

Tom toyed with the idea of a stereo or a portable TV, but in the end he decided against asking for anything. He had suspected that his father would come up with a set of wheels for Paul, Jr., to take to M.I.T. But he realized that because Paul, Jr., felt so lousy about Boss and Bandit the car was a Triumph, delivered now, instead of maybe a Chevette, delivered just before he left for college. Tom couldn't help thinking he'd be swapping Boss and Bandit for a stereo or a TV, and he couldn't bring himself to do that.

Two weeks after Paul, Jr., got the Triumph, and three weeks before he was to leave for Massachusetts, Tom happened to be looking out his bedroom window when his mother drove up in the station wagon. She got out of the car, walked around the front, and opened the passenger door. She picked up something from the seat. She held it in her arm, between her elbow and her wrist.

It looked, Tom thought, like a package of cotton wool. And then he realized what it was. It was a cat. One of those weird cats.

Tom wasn't especially fond of any kind of cat. He could tolerate a cat like Mrs. Cortell's Oscar, but he actively disliked weird, long-furred cats, and the last thing he wanted around the house was a cat with fluffy fur that looked like a roll of bandage cotton.

What his mother had done, obviously—since he and Paul, Jr., and their father agreed that they didn't want any more dogs around—was buy a cat. She meant well, but he would have nothing to do with it. It would be her own private weird cat.

"Tom!" his mother called from the foot of the stairs.

"I'm busy!" he shouted back.

"Come down here!" she ordered. It was her "I will be obeyed" tone of voice. It drew Tom from his room and to the top of the stairs.

Mrs. Lockwood was standing on the landing, stroking the white-furred cat she was holding in her arm. She was cooing to it. There was something about cats, Tom thought, that made women coo.

She looked up at him and smiled. "What do you think?" she asked.

"It'll probably sharpen its claws on your new drapes," Tom said.

She gave him a look of confusion, and then very carefully picked up the fluffy ball of fur and extended it to him.

"I don't like cats," Tom said.

"Neither do I," she said. "I mean, I don't—" Then she understood what he thought. "This is a *dog*," she said.

"You've got to be kidding."

She thrust the bundle of fur at him. He had no choice but to take it.

"Have I got the right side up?" Tom asked. "I don't see any eyes."

"They're right over the nose," his mother said. "The nose is that black thing in the middle."

He could feel a tiny heart beating in excitement, and then he realized the excitement was fear. He held the dog against his neck and stroked its back.

"What is this? One of those fuzzy mutts that lay around on old ladies' laps and eat chocolates?"

Mrs. Lockwood laughed. "Not unless it's a very large old lady," she said. "He's an Old English sheepdog."

"A what?"

"Remember the Disney movie, *The Shaggy DA*?" Mrs. Lockwood asked. "One of those."

Tom remembered the movie. The shaggy dog had been nearly as large as the movie actors.

"Do you know that for sure?" Tom asked. "Or is that what the man told you after you told him you didn't want to buy the Brooklyn Bridge?"

"He comes with a pedigree as long as your arm," Mrs.

Lockwood said. "That is a genuine Shaggy DA-type Old English sheepdog."

"Then it must be a brand-new one," Tom said. "How old is it?"

The dog was squirming against him now, no longer afraid, licking his ear. He picked it up and held it out in front of him. A tiny pink tongue came out and licked the tip of his nose.

"He's just a baby," Mrs. Lockwood said.

"No fooling?" Tom mocked her.

"His mother rejected him," she went on. "They've been feeding him by hand. They didn't want me to take him, because he's only five weeks old. I told them I'd raised three kids from the time they were a day old, and I was confident that I could handle this thing."

"His mother rejected him?" Tom pursued.

"That happens sometimes," she said. "She simply refused to let him nurse or have anything to do with him. Anyway, I've got him. Should I take him back?"

"Oh, no," Tom said. "What do we feed him?"

"I got some stuff from a vet on the faculty," she said. "Dog Pablum, I guess."

They took the puppy into the kitchen, put him on the table, and poured the contents of the can the vet had given Mrs. Lockwood into a saucer. The puppy would have nothing to do with it at first. Tom dipped his finger into the saucer and then offered his finger to the puppy. The puppy licked his finger hungrily.

Tom very gently pushed the hair away from one of the puppy's eyes. A surprisingly large, pale-blue eye looked at him.

"Well, there is a dog in there, after all," he said. Then: "To hell with your mother, hound. I'll take care of you."

Mrs. Lockwood smiled.

Dr. Lockwood came home before Paul, Jr. Tom was watching a "Star Trek" rerun on television. He had seen the segment so often he nearly knew the dialogue by heart.

"What the hell is that?" Dr. Lockwood said, pointing to the seven-inch ball of fluff asleep on Tom's lap.

"We don't know, actually," Tom said. "But it's come to live with us."

"What is it?"

"It's a dog," Tom said. "An Old English sheepdog."

"It looks like an Old English dust mop. Where did it come from?"

"Mom bought it."

"You're sure it's a dog? How can you tell?"

"I trust my mommy," Tom said. "If my mommy says it's a dog, it's a dog."

"Caroline," Dr. Lockwood called. "Did you pay real money for this walking dust mop? Or is Tom putting me on?"

"I'd hate to tell you how much I paid for him," Mrs. Lockwood said. "But I did it and I'm glad."

"I thought we agreed there'd be no more dogs."

"This isn't a dog, it's a dust mop," Tom said.

"Anyway, it's—*he's* mine," Mrs. Lockwood said. "The three of you can walk around here with your jaws hanging down to your knees, but I don't intend to. I want a dog around here, and I bought one, and that closes the subject."

"But why a—what did you say, Old English sheepdog? What good are they?"

"For one thing, they don't roam," Mrs. Lockwood said. "They're people dogs. They don't hunt anything. They're obedient, easy to train, splendid watchdogs, and very good with children."

"When did you become a walking encyclopedia on dogs?"

"Dr. Harte told me all about them."

"Who's he?"

"He's the vet who gave me the Pablum. He's on the faculty of the veterinarian college."

38

"Specializing in Old English sheepdogs?"

"No. He teaches veterinary surgery. I asked him about dogs, and that's what he told me."

"It just came up in conversation?"

"No, I went and asked him. I knew that if I waited for you guys to go get another dog, we'd never get one. And I wanted to make sure I got the right kind. Also, I thought he'd be more helpful than our old vet."

"The mountain labored," Dr. Lockwood said, "and brought forth a dust mop with legs."

"If you can't say something nice about my dog, don't say anything at all," Mrs. Lockwood said.

"Okay, okay," Dr. Lockwood said. "If you feel you're old enough to have a lapdog, be my guest."

Mrs. Lockwood laughed.

"What's so funny?"

"They're not lapdogs," she said. "They're too big for lapdogs."

"How big do they get?"

"Some of them weigh well over a hundred pounds," Mrs. Lockwood said.

"A *hundred* pounds?" Dr. Lockwood asked, in shock.

"And some of them even more. Dr. Harte says it's still too early for him to know but he wouldn't be surprised if this turned out to be a really big one."

"How big is a really big one?"

"A hundred twenty-five pounds, maybe more," she said.

Dr. Lockwood reached down and picked the puppy off Tom's lap. He held it up in front of him, pushed the hair out of its eyes, and examined it closely. The puppy tried to lick his nose.

"I'll believe a hundred twenty-five pounds if and when I see it," he said. He nuzzled the puppy. "Who ever heard of a hundred-twenty-five-pound lapdog?"

The puppy squirmed and whined.

"He's a splendid judge of character, apparently," Mrs. Lockwood said. "He doesn't do that when I pick him up."

Dr. Lockwood gave him back to Tom.

"What are you going to call it?" he asked.

"Dust Mop," Tom said. "Or how about Precious, if he's a lapdog?"

"Killer," Dr. Lockwood said. "Or Fang."

"Precious Killer," Tom said.

"Killer Dust Mop," Dr. Lockwood said.

"His name is going to be Prince," Mrs. Lockwood said.

"*Prince?*" Dr. Lockwood repeated.

"I always wanted a dog named Prince," Mrs. Lockwood said. "And now I've got one."

"You can call him Prince if you want to," Dr. Lockwood said, "but as far as I'm concerned, his name is Precious."

"I don't think that's nice, Paul," Mrs. Lockwood said. "You're making fun of him."

"Nobody, Caroline," Dr. Lockwood said, "makes fun of a dog that weighs a hundred twenty-five pounds."

"Where," Tom asked rhetorically, "does a hundred-twenty-five-pound Old English sheepdog sleep?"

Dr. Lockwood had heard the old joke.

"Any place he wants to," he said.

Mrs. Lockwood had not heard the joke.

"Don't be silly," she said. "We'll get a box for him, and some newspapers, and until he's housebroken, he sleeps in the kitchen."

"Mommy doesn't love you, Precious," Tom said. "Mommy wants you to sleep on the kitchen floor."

"I'm not his mommy," Mrs. Lockwood said, taking the puppy from Tom. "His name is not Precious, and you two are starting to make me regret bringing him home."

She held the puppy against her neck. A tiny pink tongue came out and licked her ear.

"He's really a little doll, isn't he?" she asked.

C H A P T E R   5

WHEN PAUL, JR., CAME HOME THAT DAY, Tom took a picture of the puppy, posing him in one of Paul, Jr.'s tennis shoes. He just fit inside, which proved, Dr. Lockwood said, that the puppy was a very small hound, indeed, or that Paul, Jr., had very large feet.

The puppy started to cry after everybody went upstairs to bed and left him alone in the kitchen. Mrs. Lockwood gave everybody a speech: The puppy would cry. It was perfectly all right to feel sorry for him, but giving in to his plea for pity by either going to comfort him or taking him upstairs into a bedroom was the worst possible thing they could do for him. He would have to understand immediately that whining was going to get him nowhere, or soon he would become uncontrollable.

The speech was unnecessary. Ten minutes after he had been left alone, he stopped whining and went to sleep. In the morning they found that he had somehow managed to get out of the corrugated paper box they had carefully turned into a bed for him and had slept on the rug in front of the sink. He had also carefully avoided soiling the newspaper that had been arranged around the corrugated box in case he got out of it. He had answered the call of nature on the linoleum in front of the sliding glass door that opened onto the patio.

"I feel like a monster," Mrs. Lockwood confessed, after she had given the puppy his first lesson in social behavior by telling him he was a bad boy and then taking him out onto the grass.

41

"He looks bigger this morning," Tom announced. That was obviously absurd. A dog could not grow visibly larger overnight. Tom concluded that because he'd slept on the fuzzy rug in front of the sink, the puppy's fur had somehow been fluffed up, making him appear larger.

Two minutes after he had been banished to the backyard, the puppy was back at the door, begging to get in.

"Isn't that sweet?" Mrs. Lockwood said. "He already knows where he belongs."

"What it is, Caroline," Dr. Lockwood said, as he slid the door open, "is that Precious has already figured out this is the dining room."

"His name is Prince," Mrs. Lockwood said.

"Here, Precious," Dr. Lockwood said, and made a shrill noise by pressing his lips together and blowing. The ball of fur cocked his head and then trotted over to him.

"You see?" Dr. Lockwood said triumphantly.

"If you keep that up," Mrs. Lockwood said, "he'll think his name really is Precious."

"We keep telling you it is," Dr. Lockwood said.

"I am not going to have a large dog named Precious," she said firmly.

"If Mrs. Cortell can have a cat named Oscar, we can have a dog named Precious," Dr. Lockwood said.

The Precious/Prince controversy lasted two weeks, until Barbara Lockwood came home for the weekend, scooped up the puppy, held his soft white fur against her face, and said, "Isn't he precious."

"We think so," Tom said. "Mother insists he's Prince."

"Prince?" Barbara asked incredulously.

"You call him whatever you want," Mrs. Lockwood said somewhat sharply. "I'm going to call him Prince."

And that's what happened, except when Mrs. Lockwood forgot herself and called him Precious, which after a while she did consistently.

Several weeks later, Paul, Jr., got into the Triumph and

drove off to college in Massachusetts. By that time, it was clear that the puppy had grown. It became even more obvious the day the picture they'd taken of him with Paul, Jr., who was holding him so that he wouldn't slip off the hood of the Triumph, was compared with the picture they'd taken of Precious the day they'd gotten him. He was at least three times, and probably four times, as large as he had been when Mrs. Lockwood had walked up to the house with Precious in her hand.

That very night, Precious decided he'd had enough of sleeping on the rug in front of the kitchen sink. When Tom—who had fallen into the habit of jumping out of bed the moment he woke, so that he could rush downstairs and put Precious out in the backyard before it was necessary to clean up after him—opened his bedroom door and stepped into the upstairs hallway, he stepped on Precious.

Precious naturally yipped in pain and outrage. Tom scooped up the puppy and comforted him, carrying him quickly downstairs. He thought he knew what had happened. They kept Precious in the kitchen by closing the door from the kitchen to the dining room, and by barring the passageway from the kitchen to the foyer with a sheet of scrap plywood. Precious, Tom decided, had bumped against the plywood accidentally, knocked it down, and then gone exploring.

But when he got downstairs, he found the sheet of plywood in place. Precious had jumped over it. There was no other possible explanation. He had not only jumped over it, but he'd done so like a hurdles racer, clearing it without touching it. If he had touched it, it would have fallen down.

After Precious had communed with nature, Tom tested his theory. He left the plywood barrier in place, went into the living room, and called Precious. Effortlessly, the puppy leaped over the plywood and came trotting happily into the living room.

What to do now that Precious had, as Dr. Lockwood put

it, found the key to the jail cell was discussed at breakfast. Precious was really too large to be a house dog, Dr. Lockwood said. He was large enough to sleep outside. Dr. Lockwood decided to call the plant and have Colonel Switzer get the carpentry shop to build a doghouse. A station wagon was scheduled to come down from the plant that afternoon, anyway, and the courier would just have to drive a panel truck, instead of the station wagon he usually drove, and bring the doghouse with him.

"He's not old enough to sleep outside by himself," Mrs. Lockwood said.

"Well, unless someone volunteers to sleep out there with him, he's going to have to," Dr. Lockwood said.

"He's not big enough," Mrs. Lockwood protested.

"Not this morning, he's not," Dr. Lockwood said. "But the way he's growing, he will be by suppertime."

The carpentry shop at Wallwood Microtronics was primarily responsible for building the crates in which the firm's delicate electronic equipment was shipped around the world. It was very well equipped and staffed with highly skilled carpenters, who worked under Colonel Switzer's supervision. Despite this, however, the doghouse did not arrive when it was supposed to.

Colonel Switzer telephoned to say they hadn't had plans for a doghouse right at hand. And even though he had found "suitable" plans and everybody had set to work (Dr. Lockwood was, after all, the boss), there was just no way they could finish the doghouse in a matter of hours.

Furthermore, Colonel Switzer told Dr. Lockwood on the telephone, if they were going to do this, he wanted to do it right. He wanted to come up with something nicer than a raw plywood box. Instead of using bare plywood for a roof, he wanted to shingle it. The colonel said he had shingled his beach house with cedar shakes and had just about enough shakes left over to do the doghouse. What he proposed to do was have the driver of the courier station wagon go by his beach house, pick up the cedar shakes, and bring them back to the plant. He would be able to send the finished, shingle-roofed doghouse to Dr. Lockwood when the courier made his scheduled trip on Friday. Friday was three days away. Could Dr. Lockwood do without the doghouse until then?

"That'll be fine, Colonel," Dr. Lockwood replied. "I owe you one."

That left the question of where Precious would sleep that night, and the next night, and the night after that, until his doghouse arrived.

"Well, he can't sleep in the corridor," Mrs. Lockwood said.

"What do you propose?" Dr. Lockwood said.

"I saw a dog bed in the shopping mall," she replied.

"A dog *bed?*" Dr. Lockwood asked.

"It's an oversized pillow. Canvas, or denim, or some-thing," she explained. "And stuffed with cedar shavings. That's supposed to kill both odor and fleas."

"Then why don't they call it a dog pillow?" Dr. Lockwood asked. "'Bed' sounds as if it has a headboard and a mattress."

"You'll have to ask the people who make it, dear," Mrs. Lockwood said.

"And you intend to buy one of those things?"

"Until we get the doghouse," Mrs. Lockwood said, "we can put it in Paul, Jr.'s room. Precious can sleep there. And when the doghouse comes, we can put the pillow in the doghouse."

Mrs. Lockwood picked up Tom at school. Precious was on the front seat beside her. She told Tom she was afraid that the puppy would be sick, as it was his first ride in a car since she'd brought him home. There were newspapers on the seat and on the floor, and a roll of paper towels under the armrest.

Precious did not get sick. He was having the time of his life. He stood up on the seat and pressed his nose to the window.

They went first to the shopping mall. Tom and the dog waited in the car until Mrs. Lockwood had bought and paid for the dog bed, and then Tom went inside to get it, while his mother stayed with Precious.

"You won't believe what he did," his mother said when Tom returned. "There was a car next to us, and when its owner opened the door, Precious barked at him. He was protecting me!"

"He probably wanted to play," Tom replied.

"I'm telling you, Tom," she insisted, "he barked. He was trying to protect me."

"He's a puppy."

"He was protecting me," she said firmly.

Then they drove to the university, where Dr. Harte, of the College of Veterinary Medicine, examined the puppy and gave him several injections against disease and parasites. It was the first time Tom had met Dr. Harte, and he liked him. He decided his mother had been smart to switch vets.

Tom asked Dr. Harte about Precious's behavior. He was surprised when Dr. Harte told him that his mother was probably right, that the dog had been protecting her.

"He's a shepherd," Dr. Harte said, "bred to protect a flock of sheep. In the beginning, this strain of dog probably showed a natural shepherding instinct. And then, for hundreds of years, the dogs were bred to take advantage of this instinct. The instinct is very strong. This little fella has never seen a sheep, most likely, but his instincts tell him that what he's supposed to do is protect something. He *was* protecting your mother."

"See, wiseguy?" Mrs. Lockwood said to Tom. "I told you."

"Okay, so I was wrong," Tom said.

"It may get to be a problem later on," Dr. Harte said. "Sometimes dogs take their responsibilities too seriously."

"I don't understand," Mrs. Lockwood said.

"He may decide to protect you from Tom, or from your husband," Dr. Harte said.

"And how do we handle that?" she asked.

"First with gentle discipline, and then with very firm discipline, and then, when all else fails, with a two by four," Dr. Harte said.

"You're kidding, of course," Mrs. Lockwood said sharply, as the dog squirmed in her arm so that he could lick her face.

"No, not really," Dr. Harte said. "That cuddly ball of fur is going to grow into a powerful animal weighing a hundred pounds, probably more. You can never let him forget where he fits in the scheme of things, that you're the boss."

"Oh, he's not going to bite anybody," Mrs. Lockwood said. "You yourself told me that dogs bite because they're afraid. This one is treated like a baby. He'll never have anything to be afraid of."

"Of course not," Dr. Harte said quietly.

Tom looked at him closely. It wasn't, he saw, that Dr. Harte agreed with his mother. He just didn't want to argue with her.

They drove home, and Tom carried the dog bed upstairs. They put it in Paul, Jr.'s room, which was at the end of the upstairs corridor, moving a bedside table out of the way so there would be room for it.

Precious sat and watched them and, when they were finished, went over to examine the bed. He sniffed it suspiciously, pushed it with his nose, and then walked out of the room.

"I don't think he's too thrilled with his bed, Mom," Tom said.

"He doesn't know what it is," Mrs. Lockwood replied.

Before Tom went to bed that night, he tried to make Precious settle down in the dog bed. Precious would have nothing to do with it. He wouldn't even stay in the bed when Tom put him in the middle of it.

Mrs. Lockwood brought his food and water bowls upstairs and placed them beside the dog bed. "He'll get the idea from having his food and water here," she said. "That this is his place, and that he belongs here."

Precious didn't get the idea at all.

"The trouble with him," Dr. Lockwood said, "is that he's intelligent, and he's already figured out that he can do just about what he pleases. Tomorrow, Tom, you really start training him. The first thing you teach him is 'stay.'"

"He's not old enough for that," Mrs. Lockwood protested.

"He's old enough," Dr. Lockwood said firmly.

Tom went to bed, and to sleep, but his parents woke him up after they got ready for bed, because Precious still hadn't settled down.

"Let's just close the door on him," Mrs. Lockwood said. "That'll give him the idea."

"Let's just let him make up his own mind," Dr. Lockwood countered. "Tom's in bed. We're going to bed. He'll have no place else to go. Logically, he'll go where the food is."

Tom heard his parents' door close. Then he closed his own door. There was silence afterward. And then there came the sound of Precious scratching at his door and whining. He didn't whine loudly, and as determined as his scratching was, Tom didn't think it made enough noise to wake his parents. It didn't, and after no more than a minute, there was absolute silence.

Precious finally understood. Everybody else had gone to bed, and that's what he was expected to do.

When Tom opened his door the next morning, Precious was standing there, wide awake, wagging his whole rear end and whimpering in delight. Tom stooped over and picked him up. The carpet under his foot was warm. Tom went into Paul, Jr.'s room and laid his hand on the dog bed. It was ice cold. Precious had slept right outside Tom's door, with water, food, and a $49.95 cedar-shavings-filled dog bed ten feet away.

The doghouse arrived the next day. Tom had suspected it would not be an ordinary doghouse, because of Colonel Switzer, but he did not expect what they unloaded from the white truck with the Wallwood Microtronics insignia on the doors.

"That's absurd," Dr. Lockwood said.

"It's beautiful!" Mrs. Lockwood said.

"Beautiful *and* absurd," Dr. Lockwood said.

The doghouse had been built from a photograph of a house Colonel Switzer had seen in a magazine. Tom had expected a flat roof. The doghouse had a mansard roof. He had expected plywood walls. The doghouse was entirely covered with cedar shakes. He had expected a square hole, over which he thought he would nail an old blanket, for a door. The doghouse had a door with a window, hung from a spring hinge, so the dog could push it open in either direction, going in or out. There were realistic-looking chimneys at each end of the roof. Tom, when he got on his knees and peered in, would not have been surprised to find a fireplace inside. There was no fireplace, but neither were there the raw walls he expected. The doghouse was insulated, and there was actually an attic with an exhaust fan. And there was something else, a sign, designed to be stuck in the lawn, identifying the occupant.

The only one who was not impressed with the dog mansion was Precious. He eyed Tom suspiciously, as Tom put the dog bed inside the house. He then refused to go into it. Finally, Tom got on his hands and knees and pushed the dog inside. Precious stayed there just long enough to figure out how to get out. Then he circled it twice, sniffed it once, and raised his leg.

"I'm glad Colonel Switzer isn't here for that opinion," Dr. Lockwood said.

"You know very well," Mrs. Lockwood said, "that that's just a canine characteristic. Males mark their property that way."

They tried to leave Precious outside that night, to force him to use the doghouse, but he patiently, almost politely, scratched at the door, until finally Dr. Lockwood gave in to him. Then, and thereafter, Precious slept on the carpet in front of Tom's room.

A couple of days later, the words "For Rent" appeared on the sign. Mrs. Lockwood suspected Tom's father, but he professed innocence.

C H A P T E R 6

TOM LOCKWOOD HAD NOTICED WITHOUT MUCH surprise that the "For Sale" sign on the house three doors away from the Lockwoods' had come down. Houses on Palm Drive sold quickly whenever they went on the market. His father had explained it simply: There was only so much shoreline, or property on the water, and there was something deep in the human animal that made him want to be close to the water. There were more people who wanted to live next to the water than there were places there to live.

Two weeks after the sign had come down, moving vans appeared, and the people who had lived there moved out. Tom had had only a waving acquaintance with them, and there was no sense of loss. Two days after they moved out, the new owners moved in. Tom paid more attention to this development. It was possible, if not likely, that the new people would have a daughter his age, who would be not only good-looking but eager to make the acquaintance of someone who could show her how to fish and otherwise make her a part of the community.

For about ten minutes, he thought that fortune had finally smiled on him, for a female did appear, an attractive female with blond hair who had just smiled and waved at him as he'd ridden past on his bike on the way home from school. He gulped down a large glass of milk, combed his hair, and rode back down the street.

The attractive female was on the front lawn now, and she was even better-looking than he'd thought after just a glancc. He also saw that she wore a wedding and an engagement ring on the third finger of her left hand. It would have been nice if he could have just ridden on by, but in his enthusiasm he had waved cheerfully at her before seeing the wedding ring, and she had waved back and stepped to the curb. There was nothing to do but stop.

"Hi," she said. "I'm Joanna Haynes. I guess we're now neighbors."

"Yes, ma'am," Tom replied. "I guess we are. I'm Tom Lockwood. I live down there in the house with the fence."

"I noticed," she said. "I wanted to talk to you about the fence."

He wondered what she meant by that. She let him know immediately. "Could you tell me who built it for you? We're going to need one like it."

"I don't really know who built it," Tom confessed. "The colonel arranged for it."

"The colonel?"

"Colonel Switzer," Tom explained. "He works with my father. He's an engineer, and when my dad decided we needed a fence, he asked the colonel to arrange to have it built."

"Oh," she said. "I see. I don't want to be nosey, but do you think you could find out for me? I walked up and took a look at it the day we decided to buy the house, and it's just what we need. The truth is, we have a dog problem."

"Excuse me?"

"We have a dog," she said, and gestured toward the house, "with what my husband calls a Napoleon complex."

Tom looked at the house. In the center of the bay window in front, he saw the head of a Doberman pinscher. The dog's head was cocked to one side, and his ears were erect. He was obviously fascinated with what was going on on the lawn.

"A Napoleon complex?" Tom parroted.

52

"He likes to fight," Mrs. Haynes explained. "He doesn't like other dogs."

Tom looked at the Doberman again. He didn't look vicious. He actually looked just the opposite, like a nice dog that didn't like being locked in the house when his mistress was outside but was patiently waiting for her to finish whatever she had to do.

"Come on," Mrs. Haynes said. "I'll introduce you."

They walked up the lawn to the front door. The Doberman watched without moving until he was sure of their intentions, and then disappeared from the window. Mrs. Haynes opened the front door. The dog was waiting for them inside, his short, stubby tail seemingly wagging the whole rear end of his body.

"Sit!" Mrs. Haynes said. The dog immediately sat down.

"Tom," Mrs. Haynes said, "this is Bonaparte. Bonaparte, this is Tom."

Bonaparte offered Tom his paw. He was a beautiful animal. His dark-brown coat was slick and shiny, and his eyes were bright and intelligent.

"How are you, pooch?" Tom said, shaking the dog's paw.

"He loves people," Mrs. Haynes said. "Unfortunately, he doesn't like other dogs, especially male dogs."

"He seems like a nice dog," Tom said.

"He's a *wonderful* dog," she said. "Unless you happen to be a boy dog yourself. Then he's a real stinker. We really need a fence to keep him in. A fence like yours, one he can't possibly get through."

"Maybe my mother knows who built our fence," Tom said. "If you'd like, I'll ask her."

"I wish you would," Mrs. Haynes said.

"I'll do it right now," Tom said.

"Say so long to Tom, Bonaparte," Mrs. Haynes said. Bonaparte offered Tom his paw again. He seemed like a very friendly dog, Tom thought, and wondered if Mrs. Haynes was exaggerating about his tendency to fight.

Mrs. Lockwood was home when Tom got there, and when he told her of his conversation with Mrs. Haynes, she took a bottle of wine from the closet. Then she went to call on Mrs. Haynes, to welcome her to the neighborhood.

Ten minutes later, she had returned with Mrs. Haynes. The Hayneses' phone hadn't been connected, and to find out who had built the fence, they had to call Colonel Switzer.

Precious was as happy to meet Mrs. Haynes as Bonaparte had been to meet Tom, but no way near so well mannered. He licked her face and hands and tried to jump all over her. Tom vowed then and there to teach Precious some manners. If Bonaparte could sit politely and offer his paw to a newcomer, there was no reason Precious couldn't do the same thing.

Mrs. Haynes wasn't angry about Precious's bad manners. She said he was adorable. She also seemed very relieved to hear that Precious was rarely outside the Lockwoods' fence.

Mrs. Lockwood reached Colonel Switzer on the telephone and got the name of the fence contractor for Mrs. Haynes. Shortly afterward, Mrs. Haynes left.

As soon as she'd walked out the door, Tom took Precious and a carton of dog biscuits to his room. In thirty minutes, Precious was offering his paw on command. Every time he offered his paw, he was rewarded with a piece of dog biscuit. Tom was delighted with how quickly Precious had gotten the idea.

Three days later, the fence contractor appeared at the Haynes house, and by the afternoon of the next day, the Hayneses had a fence nearly identical to the Lockwoods' around their lot. Mrs. Lockwood wondered aloud if she had made a mistake in not telling Mrs. Haynes that her other neighbors were not fond of fences.

"I don't understand the objection," Dr. Lockwood said. "Fences keep the dogs at home, off other people's lawns."

"It's just that fences are so ugly," Mrs. Lockwood argued.

"For maybe ten thousand dollars," Dr. Lockwood replied, "we could take the fence down and replace it with an ivy-covered brick wall."

"Don't be sarcastic," Mrs. Lockwood said.

"I think the Hayneses are trying hard to be good neighbors," he said. "And I think the fence haters are unreasonable."

Mrs. Lockwood changed the subject. "Precious is still a puppy," she said. "Maybe it would be a good idea if we introduced him to Bonaparte, to see if they'll make friends now. Joanna Haynes says that Bonaparte really gets nasty. But that's probably with grown dogs, not puppies."

"It wouldn't hurt to try, I suppose," Dr. Lockwood said.

The experiment was a disaster. Polite and gentle Bonaparte started growling the instant he saw Precious coming up the street. Mrs. Haynes was able to make him behave, to sit down, but he laid his ears back against his skull, bared his teeth, and growled deeply, if softly, in his throat.

"Precious is just a baby, Bonaparte," Mrs. Haynes said. "Don't be such a louse!"

Tom was afraid of Bonaparte's behavior, and he wondered if Precious was stupid, for Precious didn't seem at all concerned. He walked up to Bonaparte's fence and put his nose against it. His rear end wasn't wagging, and he didn't yelp happily, but neither did he seem to understand that the other dog actively disliked him.

"Well, Tom," Mrs. Haynes said, "we tried. I guess the only thing we can do is make sure we keep them apart."

When Tom turned and started leading Precious back down the block, and Mrs. Haynes started to go into her house, Bonaparte decided that this meant he had permission to stop sitting down. All of his teeth now showing, growling so loudly and so menacingly that Tom was actually frightened, he raced to the fence and jumped up against it, trying to get at Precious. Mrs. Haynes came running back down the lawn, shouting "Down! Down!"

Shocked and frightened, and without thinking about it, Tom stooped over to pick up Precious, to protect him from Bonaparte.

When Mrs. Haynes got close enough to Bonaparte to scream in his ear, Bonaparte stopped trying to get over the fence and at Precious. Eventually, still growling through bared teeth, he sat down.

"You better get Precious out of here, Tom," Mrs. Haynes called. "I'm so sorry."

"It's all right," Tom said, and headed home, carrying Precious. He had gone about twenty yards when he realized two things. First, that picking up Precious would have done absolutely no good if Bonaparte had been able to get over the fence. And second, that Precious wasn't acting like a terrified puppy. Precious's body was as stiff as a board; all of his muscles were tensed. And Precious wasn't whining. He was growling. Precious wasn't afraid. Precious, Tom thought, was stupid. He was perfectly willing to fight Bonaparte, who was three or four times his size.

Tom carried Precious all the way home. He was afraid that if he put him on the ground, Precious would race back to the Hayneses' fence and answer Bonaparte's challenge.

At supper, he told his father what had happened.

"There's only one solution to the problem," Dr. Lockwood said. "Just make sure the two of them don't get together."

"And I've got to train him to make damned sure he comes when I call him," Tom said.

"Don't swear," Mrs. Lockwood said.

"You damned well better," Dr. Lockwood said. "I have a

sneaking suspicion that Precious has a tendency to be just as hardheaded as Bonaparte."

"Now," Mrs. Lockwood demanded, defending Precious, "why do you have to say something like that?"

"Because he took a nip at me," Dr. Lockwood said.

"He did?" she asked, surprised. "Why?"

"What did you do?" Tom asked.

Dr. Lockwood answered both questions in one sentence. "I got a little too close to his food," he said, "and I threw him as far as I could across the backyard."

"You did *what?*" Mrs. Lockwood asked.

"I threw him across the backyard," Dr. Lockwood said. "A dog, and I don't care what you do to him, short of tormenting him, has no right to snap at his master. I was teaching him that lesson."

"You could have hurt him," Mrs. Lockwood said, shocked and angry.

"I certainly hope I got his attention," Dr. Lockwood said. "Or would you rather I let him grow up to act like Bonaparte?"

"You could have hurt him," Mrs. Lockwood repeated, but without much conviction.

The next day Tom went to the school library, looking for a book on how to train an Old English sheepdog. There was nothing in the school library at all, so he went to the public library on the way home. There was a book there on Old English sheepdogs, but it was more of an advertisement than a training manual. It said that they were very large and faithful dogs, easy to train and especially good with children. Most of the book was filled with pictures of Old English sheepdogs in one sweet, charming pose after another. All the dogs in the photographs were spotless and had their hair combed out. The book, however, had nothing to say about taking care of the dogs' hair.

Tom wound up at the bookstore. The woman who ran it

showed him two books. One was written expressly for people who wanted to show their Old English sheepdogs in American Kennel Club competition. There were several chapters on grooming, and Tom, reading them, was smugly pleased that he had figured out how to comb Precious's hair by himself. He had found a brush in the hardware store, with stainless steel bristles set in a rubber backing. Using that and a wide-toothed plastic comb, he had been able to keep Precious's hair free of snags. He had bought exactly what the book on showing Old English sheepdogs recommended.

The second book the bookstore owner showed him was on the training of bird dogs. Precious wasn't anything like Boss and Bandit in feature, size, shape, or personality, but he was, Tom reasoned, a dog, and, looks aside, dogs couldn't be all that different from one another. He bought *How to Train a Bird Dog* and paid for it himself, instead of charging it to his father (who was, Dr. Lockwood said, the bookstore's major source of income) and running the risk of having his father ask him if he didn't know the difference between a bird dog and an Old English sheepdog.

There was a good deal of very sound advice in the book. The man who wrote it knew what he was talking about, and obviously loved dogs. He said that if he is smart, a dog will resist training until he is absolutely convinced that he's going to be trained whether or not he likes it.

As soon as Tom started to really train Precious, he realized what had happened. Precious had learned quickly that he was adorable, and that adorable meant he didn't have to do anything he didn't want to do, so long as he wagged his rear end and licked people's faces and hands.

"Don't give in!" the book counseled. "Decide what you want the dog to do, one small step at a time, and then make him do it."

The first small step, Tom decided, was actually two small steps. Precious had to be trained to come when he was called, whether or not there was something else he would

e or four times
e.

During the
ng, whacking-
ning, she often
procedure. She
at she thought
little Precious.
number two,
place and told
om's having to
t was as far as
just sat there
world who he

a collar. There
ere was. There
he didn't want
m knew where
hanging in the
Bandit. He felt
nail in the ga-
ewellin setters

neck with his
in terror when
ne choker.
nd like a traf-

n him, letting
ached the end

bered he was
histle-trained.
beginning, to

rather be doing, like sniffing at a tree; and he had to stay when and where he was told to stay, whether or not he liked that, either.

The book cautioned against giving a dog too many rewards. "A pat on the head is sufficient when he's good," the book said. "And, *usually,* telling him sternly that he's a bad boy is enough when he needs correction."

Precious was a good boy in the Lockwood yard for about thirty seconds. He came the first time Tom called him. But he was visibly disappointed that he got no piece of dog biscuit in payment. (Tom wondered how he knew Precious was disappointed. Precious couldn't talk, and you couldn't even see his eyes. There was no logical explanation, but Tom *knew.*)

When Tom told him to stay, Precious stayed about five seconds before starting to trot after Tom. Tom picked him up and carried him back to where he was supposed to stay, told him again in a firm voice to stay, and held his hand up like a traffic cop. That didn't work, either, although Tom tried it five times before giving up.

He checked the book for instructions, and, sure enough, there they were:

If calm reason fails, there are two additional steps you can take:

(1) The moment the dog starts to leave the spot where he has been ordered to stay, jump up and down like a raving maniac, shouting and waving your arms. This frequently will be enough to get him to do what he should. If it isn't:

(2) Roll up a newspaper, not too tightly. After jumping up and down and waving your arms as outlined above, whack him with the newspaper on his hindquarter. Make as much noise as possible. The idea is to scare him without hurting him.

Tom went into the kitch
paper, rolled a section of it into
with rubber bands. Then he we

He put Precious where h
"stay," and backed away from
twenty feet away, Precious start
the air, screamed an Indian wa
Scouts, and waved his arms ar
in his tracks and stayed that
jumping, screaming, and wavi
rear end wagging as if in ant
trotted over happily.

Tom scooped him up, sho
back to where he was suppose
it, he whacked him twice wit
shouted.

Precious cringed and curl
Tom backed away twenty feet,
didn't budge.

"Come!" Tom called.
Precious didn't budge.
"Come!" Tom called agai
Precious clearly had no
near his former friend, who h
started jumping in the air, wa
worse, had actually struck hi

Training Precious to stay
slightly more difficult than t
exchange for a piece of dog b
he had dreamed it would be.

even eager, to fight Bonaparte, who was thr
his size, the stupid theory seemed reasonab

Mrs. Lockwood wasn't much help
jumping-up-and-down, arm-waving, scream
with-the-newspaper stage of Precious's trai
came out onto the patio and watched the
made it plain, without saying very much, th
Tom was being cruel and heartless to helples

But toward the end of training sessio
Precious finally gave up. When Tom set him i
him to stay, he stayed. He sat there without
scream at him and without cringing. But tha
he was willing to go. When Tom called him, h
and looked at Tom as if he had no idea in th
was or what he wanted.

Until that day, Precious had never worn
had been no need for him to wear one. Now th
was no way Precious was going to move when
to, unless he was pulled by his collar. And To
to find one. There were half a dozen of them
garage, collars that had belonged to Boss and
very bad when he took a choke collar from a
rage. He still missed the matched pair of L
very much.

Precious tried to push the collar off his
paws when Tom put it on him, and he shrank
Tom fastened a thirty-foot length of cord to t

"Stay!" Tom ordered, putting up his ha
fic cop.

Precious stayed. Tom backed away fro
the cord slip through his fingers until he re
of it.

"Come!" he ordered.

Precious didn't move. Then Tom remer
doing this wrong. Boss and Bandit had been w
Dr. Lockwood had trained them, from the

come when he blew two short, sharp blasts on a whistle.

Tom dropped the cord, told Precious to "Stay!" once again, and went back to the garage to get a whistle. Taking one of the whistles down from the nail where they had been hung was even harder than taking the collar had been. He had a clear and very painful mind's-eye picture of Boss and Bandit in the field, racing back to him, tails flying, in response to whistle blasts.

He forced it from his mind. He told himself that if Boss and Bandit had learned to come happily when called, Precious would just have to do the same thing.

When he went back out to the yard, Tom saw that Precious was not where he had left him. He was in the far corner of the yard, rolling around, trying to get free of the cord tied to his collar.

"Come!" Tom called. Precious behaved as if he were stone deaf.

Tom walked toward him and found the end of the cord. He put the whistle in his mouth and blew two blasts. Then he called, "Come!"

Precious ignored him.

Tom blew the whistle twice again, called, "Come!" again, and was ignored again.

Tom did it a third time, and this time, when Precious ignored him, Tom hauled him in at the end of the cord. Precious braced his feet against the pull of the cord. Tom kept pulling. He blew two blasts on the whistle, called, "Come!" and hauled Precious to him. Precious started to yelp, more and more loudly, as Tom dragged him closer. Then he stopped bracing himself against the tug of the cord and tried to run away, yelping all the while in what sounded like absolute terror.

He made enough noise to attract Mrs. Lockwood's attention. She appeared on the patio. "What in the world are you doing to him?" she demanded.

Precious saw a friend who could help him in his trouble. Yelping even more loudly, he tried to get to Mrs. Lockwood.

Tom continued to haul Precious toward him. Precious continued to yelp for help.

"Mom, go into the house, will you, please!" Tom called.

"You're going to hurt him," she said.

"That's right. What I am is some kind of freak who gets his kicks torturing dogs," Tom said, losing his temper. "What I'm going to do next is roast him alive over a charcoal fire."

Mrs. Lockwood frowned and went into the house. Precious howled.

Tom now had had enough of Precious, too. He pulled on the cord more sharply, knocking Precious off his feet and tightening the choke collar around his neck, so that the dog had a hard time breathing. When Precious was at his feet, he picked him up, shook him, and put his nose next to the doghouse.

"Get it straight, stupid!" he shouted. "You *are* going to do it my way!"

Then he set the dog, who was trembling again, back on the lawn. "Stay, damn you!" he said, and started to back away. Precious lay down with his head between his paws. And he didn't move until Tom had reached the end of the cord.

Tom put the whistle between his lips and got a good grip on the cord. If Precious didn't come now, he was going to be dragged over on his nose.

"Come!" Tom ordered, and blew two blasts on the whistle.

Precious didn't move.

Tom was now afraid that he really would hurt him if he dragged him again. He thought it over and decided that he would have to do it, anyway. And if he was going to do it, he might as well do it right. He gripped the cord and prepared to jerk it. He blew two blasts on the whistle and called, "Come!"

Precious got to his feet and, wagging his tail, trotted happily over to Tom.

Tom dropped to his knees and hugged him. Precious licked Tom's neck and ears.

"Good boy!" Tom said, as surprised as he was pleased.

Then it occurred to him that Precious's cheerful, willing obedience might have been a fluke. He pushed Precious's rear end to the ground, told him to "Sit!" and "Stay!" and then backed away from him again, to the end of the length of cord.

Precious stayed, and he came when Tom blew the whistle.

The next step was to do the whole business without the cord.

That didn't go absolutely smoothly. Precious was aware that the collar and cord were gone. The first time Tom blew the two blasts on the whistle, Precious just looked at him. Tom's stomach sank. Then he blew the whistle again, and this time Precious came trotting to him.

"Once more," Tom said. "And that'll be all for today. I don't want to press my luck."

Tom practiced with Precious for the rest of the week and once more early Sunday morning, before he showed Precious's new training to his father. He kept increasing his distance from Precious before calling him, and ultimately, though not without trouble, he succeeded in having Precious stay even when he went out of sight.

After breakfast on Sunday, he took his father to the backyard and showed Precious off. Precious performed flawlessly for Tom, but when Dr. Lockwood tried to take him through the routine, Precious, rather than staying, immediately ran to Tom.

"He's just a baby," Mrs. Lockwood said, defending him. "He doesn't know what you expect of him."

"You and Tom go inside," Dr. Lockwood said. "What it is, is that he doesn't know who he's supposed to listen to."

Tom and his mother went into the house and looked out the dining-room window. They saw that Precious was looking at the kitchen door, hoping that either one of them would come out. He stayed when Dr. Lockwood put him in position, but when Dr. Lockwood blew the whistle, instead of going to him, Precious headed straight for the kitchen door.

Tom and his mother smiled at each other. Then they heard Dr. Lockwood's angry voice: "*Damn* you!" he said, and when they snapped their heads back to look out the window, they saw Precious flying through the air. He landed awkwardly on his side and, yelping in pain, ran off to the far corner of the yard.

They heard the kitchen door slam open, and they ran into the kitchen. Dr. Lockwood was standing in front of the sink, running water over his hand.

"What was that all about?" Mrs. Lockwood demanded.

"He bit me," Dr. Lockwood said. "That's what it was all about. I tried to pick him up when he was at the kitchen door, and he bit me!"

"Let me see," she said, concern now in her voice. She went to the sink and took his hand in hers. "I would say that's more of a scratch than a bite," she said. "But I guess we'd better put something on it."

"If it's not a bite, that's not because he wasn't trying," Dr. Lockwood said.

"And if you didn't break his neck, or his leg, throwing him the way you did," Mrs. Lockwood replied, "it wasn't because you weren't trying."

"What I was trying to do," Dr. Lockwood said, "is convince that animal that taking bites out of people is a no-no." Then he looked at Tom. "Go see if I hurt him," he said. "But don't give him any sympathy."

Tom found Precious behind the fancy doghouse. He was lying down, his muzzle resting on his paws. It was evident that he knew that he had done something wrong and was in trouble. He didn't get up or even move.

"I hope you realize you're in trouble," Tom said to him.

Precious started to crawl over to him, and, for a moment, Tom was afraid that he had been hurt and couldn't move otherwise. But when he got to Tom, he changed into a sitting position and offered Tom his paw.

"You don't have to apologize to me," Tom said. "Yon Olde Man's the one who's mad at you." Tom let go of Precious's paw. Precious handed it to him again. Tom shook it again, then said, "Come on, you can tell the Olde Man you're sorry."

He walked to the house, and Precious followed him.

"Is he all right?" Dr. Lockwood said. Mrs. Lockwood was painting his hand with Merthiolate.

"He's the original repentant sinner," Tom said.

Precious hid behind Tom's legs, peering around them at Dr. and Mrs. Lockwood.

"Look at that!" Mrs. Lockwood said. "You can tell he's sorry."

Dr. Lockwood dropped to his knees.

"Learned your lesson, have you?" he asked. Precious offered his paw. Dr. Lockwood shook it.

"Okay, Precious," he said. "We're friends again. I really hope that getting thrown through the air got through to you."

"What would you have done if you'd hurt him?" Mrs. Lockwood asked.

"What would you have done if he'd really bitten me?" Dr. Lockwood replied.

"He was frightened," she said. "You frightened him. The only reason he nipped at you was because he was frightened."

"I hope you're right," he said.

For the rest of the day, Precious did not leave Tom's side. When they ate dinner, Precious lay under the table and went to sleep with his head on Tom's foot.

Mrs. Lockwood remarked that he really was a good dog,

that he had quickly learned he was not allowed to beg at the table.

"He doesn't have to beg," Dr. Lockwood said. "He just has to wait until he's reached his full growth. Then he'll be able to help himself to whatever he wants, and we'll be afraid to say anything to him."

Precious continued to grow at a remarkable rate. By the time Paul, Jr., came home from M.I.T. for the Christmas holidays, he weighed sixty-five pounds and was so big that when Tom stood him on the scale to weigh him, he couldn't see the numbers. And when Tom held him while Paul, Jr., got on his hands and knees to read the scale, he felt how tough and heavy Precious's body was getting underneath all his fluffy hair.

When Paul, Jr., had walked into the house, for a moment Precious hadn't remembered him. He had stood up and leaned against Tom's leg and wouldn't go anywhere near Paul, Jr., until Paul, Jr., had gotten on his hands and knees and approached him. That had seemed to trigger Precious's memory, for his rear end had started to wag and he had run to Paul, Jr., and crawled all over him. After that, he seldom left Paul, Jr.'s side, and Tom realized, feeling a little silly about it, that he was jealous.

Paul, Jr., took Precious with him in the Triumph, and that was another indication of how large, and how quickly, he had grown. Precious was able to stand on his back paws and rest his front paws on top of the windshield, and ride around with his head above the windshield, the wind whipping the hair back, so that you could see his big blue eyes.

Precious misbehaved only twice during the Christmas holidays. On Christmas morning, when he discovered that a new tree had miraculously appeared in the living room, he walked directly to it, raised his leg, and marked it conspicuously so that other dogs would understand that it was within his property line.

Everyone but Mrs. Lockwood thought this was hilarious. Even Barbara, though she'd been greeted on arrival by a rambunctious Precious, who had jumped on her and dirtied her dress, laughed loudly.

Tom didn't tell anyone about the second thing Precious did.

On New Year's Eve, Paul, Jr., went to a party that lasted most of the night. He would have preferred to sleep until noon or later on New Year's Day, but at about half past ten in the morning, he got a telephone call. When he didn't pick up the extension telephone in his room, Mrs. Lockwood ordered Tom upstairs to wake him up.

A little annoyed at having to serve as his brother's bellboy, Tom raced up the stairs, taking them two at a time, and started down the upstairs corridor to Paul, Jr.'s room. He was greeted, and frankly scared out of his skin, by Precious, who was standing on his toes, his teeth bared, every muscle tensed, growling deeply and menacingly in his chest, in preparation to spring.

"Hey, dummy!" Tom said. "It's me!"

It took Precious a good thirty seconds to recognize him. Then he stopped growling, came down off his toes, and walked over to Tom to lick his hand. Until he did, though, Tom, who stood frozen, afraid to move, was convinced that Precious was going to attack him.

Tom felt a little silly at being terrified of his own dog and found excuses for what had happened. Precious had been sound asleep in the corridor, and Tom had come charging up the stairs like a locomotive. The corridor light hadn't been turned on, and in the dark, and half-asleep, Precious hadn't recognized him and had therefore done what good dogs are supposed to do, protect their families from strangers who are making threatening moves.

There was a third incident while Paul, Jr., was at home, though Precious was not responsible for this one. No one had remembered to tell Paul, Jr., about the Hayneses' Bonaparte. Paul, Jr., had taken Precious for a walk around the neighborhood, and when they had walked past the Hayneses' house, Bonaparte had thrown himself at the fence in an attempt to get at Precious.

It was clear that Bonaparte had frightened Paul, Jr., as much as he had frightened Tom. Tom thought that was funny, but there was a nagging fear at the back of his mind. They had had dogs as long as he could remember, and the dogs had never really scared anyone, or acted as if they would like to tear apart another dog or bite someone. Bonaparte, like Precious, was different. Their behavior was not a pleasant thing to have to think about.

CHAPTER 8

BY THE TIME PAUL, JR., CAME HOME FOR THE summer after his freshman year, Precious weighed almost one hundred pounds. And Precious's coat was one of several reasons Tom was glad to see Paul, Jr., roll up the driveway in the Triumph. The dog's coat looked like it had grown even faster than the dog. Not only did it make him look larger than he actually was, but it also required almost daily attention to keep it from getting snagged and matted. That job had fallen to Tom because he was home alone. But now that Paul, Jr., was there, the responsibility would be shared.

When he heard the Triumph in the driveway, Precious growled and ran ahead of Tom to the side door to see who had come. Tom hesitated to open the door, half afraid that Precious might not recognize Paul, Jr. He was tempted to order the dog to stay.

Once he'd gotten over his initial hardheadedness, Precious had really learned that lesson. When he was told to stay, he stayed, no matter where he was or what was going on. He stayed in the car, on the *GIGO*, and even on the lawn. But, for reasons known only to Precious, when he was told to stay in the house, he invariably trotted quickly to the stairs, climbed halfway up, and sat down. And stayed.

Tom had concluded that, in Precious's mind, where the family slept was very important. And if they didn't want him to protect the entire house, he would do the next best thing: He would protect the upstairs, where the family slept, by stationing himself on the stairs.

71

When Paul, Jr., arrived, Precious was ready to race through the side door and protect the fort from whatever intruder was at the gates. The smart thing to do, Tom realized, would be order him to stay and send him reluctantly but surely up the stairs.

"Watch it, here comes Precious!" he called, and opened the door. Precious raced through the door, stopping about ten feet from the nose of the Triumph. He took a good look. Then he took two more steps and leaped over the passenger-side door into the seat.

He landed on Paul, Jr.'s lap, knocked him into the door, and started licking his face. Tom couldn't see very much of Paul, Jr., just a blur of fluffy fur, white from the shoulders back and black over the shoulders.

"Pity," Tom said. "I was hoping he wouldn't remember you."

The door opened, and Paul, Jr., crawled out from under the dog.

"You've been feeding him Giant Pills, obviously," Paul, Jr., said, and then dropped to his knees to smooch the dog some more. Precious's hindquarters swung happily back and forth. He knocked Paul, Jr., over on his rear end. Precious was delirious with joy at seeing him.

"Stay!" Tom called sharply. Precious, who had been standing over Paul, Jr., trying to lick his face, looked over his shoulder at Tom.

"Stay!" Tom repeated, again sharply.

Precious's rear end stopped wagging. He lowered his head and stepped off Paul, Jr., and walked sadly into the house.

"Very impressive," Paul, Jr., said. "But why?"

"I don't like to get him excited in the heat," Tom said, offering his hand to his brother, and then, when Paul, Jr., had taken it, using it to haul him to his feet. "That's an awful heavy fur coat he has to wear."

"Yeah," Paul, Jr., said. "Did you see the way he leaped over the door? You wouldn't think a dog that big could move that way."

"He's just a great big furry gazelle," Tom said dryly. "Open the trunk, and I'll give you a hand with your bags."

"Where's Mother?"

"At the university," Tom replied. "And the Olde Man is at the shop."

"Who's here, then?" Paul, Jr., asked, pointing to the Mustang in the parking area in front of the double garage.

"Just me," Tom said, savoring the moment.

"Who owns the Mustang, dummy?"

"Dad owns it. Or the company does," Tom said. "I drive it."

"Oh, that's right," Paul, Jr., said. "You are old enough for a learner's permit, aren't you?" And then he thought that over. "You're not telling me Dad bought you a car to learn on, are you?"

"I read the small print in the license manual," Tom said smugly. "The small print often has some very interesting stuff in it."

"Am I supposed to understand what you mean?" Paul, Jr., asked. Then he laughed. "Hey, look at that!"

Tom looked over his shoulder. If Precious had gone to the stairs, he certainly hadn't stayed there. He was peering around the door, as if he were afraid he would be seen and chased away.

"Come on, Precious," Paul, Jr., called, and the dog came out of the door like a shot. When he reached Paul, Jr., he went up on his hind legs, draped his front paws on Paul, Jr.'s shoulders, and started to lick his face again.

"Tell him down," Tom said, "and he'll stop that."

"Down!" Paul, Jr., said. Precious ignored him. "Down, damn it!" Paul, Jr., repeated.

"Down!" Tom called.

Precious dropped to the ground. It didn't matter, Tom decided, whose order he had obeyed. The point was that he *had* obeyed. He was still a puppy, despite his size. Old English sheepdogs didn't reach their full growth until they were nearly two years old. If one year of a dog's life was equal to seven years of a human life, then Precious was just about seven years old. For a seven-year-old, he was remarkably well behaved.

"Let's get back to the Mustang," Paul, Jr., said. "What do you mean, it belongs to the company?"

"What you're looking at is a messenger transport vehicle," Tom said. "And the messenger—"

"I won't ask you to explain yourself," Paul, Jr., said, as he handed Tom a heavy cardboard box to carry into the house. "I can see that I don't have to."

"When I went down to the state police barracks to get my learner's permit," Tom said, "I forgot that manual they give you. And when I asked for another one, they didn't have one, so they let me look at the real manual. That booklet they give you is an abridgment."

"Get to the point!"

"Paragraph thirty-six *d* says that you have to be sixteen to get a driver's license—*unless* you can prove that you have to drive in your job, and then you can have a license when you're fifteen."

"How could you prove you have to drive in your job?"

"Very easy. I do. Before I go to school in the morning, I drive down to the bus station to see what came in for the shop during the night, and then I take that by the shop. I go again after school to see what's come in, and then again at five o'clock to take stuff we're sending up to the plant."

"I don't think you're trying to put me on."

"I'm not. Dad did a study. It's a lot cheaper for the company to pay me minimum wage, four hours a day, and pay for the Mustang and the bus, than it was for them to send a

74

courier between the plant and the shop every other day. It's also quicker."

"How come Dad didn't come up with this when I was in high school?"

"Dad didn't come up with it. I did."

"You just said Dad did a study."

"That was to check my study," Tom said. "He tried to disprove my theory. When he couldn't do that, I had him hooked."

Paul, Jr., didn't want to hear any more of this. He changed the subject. "With you gone all day and Mom at the university, what happens to Precious?"

"He spends the day at the shop," Tom said. "Mrs. Lopez brings him their table scraps."

"Pop doesn't mind having him around the shop? Doesn't he get in the way?"

"You would be surprised how few door-to-door salesmen have the courage to open the gate in the fence when they see Precious," Tom said. "Or hear him barking. Pop thinks it's great."

"He sure looks good," Paul, Jr., said.

"Thank you," Tom said. "I'm sure that you'll be able, after a while, to do just as well."

"Meaning what?"

"Meaning now that you're home, we can take turns brushing and combing him."

"You're kidding!"

"I kid you not."

"That's your dog, little brother," Paul, Jr., said. "If he needs brushing and combing, you do it."

"Then you don't intend to use him to meet girls?"

Paul, Jr., understood Tom's meaning. He frowned at Tom. "You mean you won't lend him to me? As a small token of your brotherly love and respect?"

"After you brush him, sure," Tom said.

"I see that it is necessary to bring you down from cloud nine onto solid earth," Paul, Jr., said. "Come on, Precious, we'll go for a ride!"

Ride was one of maybe twenty words in Precious's vocabulary. He knew exactly what it meant. He jumped nimbly over the door of the Triumph and took his place in the passenger seat.

Tom realized that Paul, Jr., was rubbing his nose in the dirt by letting him know Paul, Jr., was far too exalted a personage to comb and brush a dog, and that he would enjoy Precious while leaving the labor to Tom. Tom saw red. "Stay!" he ordered.

Precious looked at him and lowered his head in unhappiness. He didn't move.

Paul, Jr., jumped behind the wheel and started the engine. He thumbed his nose at Tom.

"Precious!" Tom said, very sharply. "Stay!"

Paul, Jr., started to back down the driveway.

"Stay!" Tom called again. Precious jumped back out of the car, walked slowly and sadly to Tom, and lay down at his feet. Paul, Jr., slammed the brakes and called to him. Precious didn't move.

Tom thumbed his nose at his brother.

"You're right, he *is* my dog," he said.

"Damn you, Precious," Paul, Jr., said angrily, getting out of the car. "When I tell you to come, you come!"

Precious sat up and leaned his chest against Tom's leg.

"Come, Precious!" Paul, Jr., repeated. When Precious didn't leave Tom, Paul, Jr., moved closer. "Come, damn it!" he shouted.

All of a sudden, Precious stood up, seeming to rise on his toes. His lips curled back away from his teeth and a menacing growl began in his throat.

Paul, Jr., became frightened, but not as frightened as Tom. Tom dropped to his knees and threw his arms around

Precious's shoulders. He did it just in time. If Tom hadn't grabbed him when he had, Precious would have attacked Paul, Jr.

"What the hell was that all about?" Paul, Jr., said in a faint voice.

"He thought you were threatening me," Tom said, forcing Precious back on his haunches, comforting him, calming him down. He felt Precious's remarkably stiff muscles relax.

Precious went limp and his lips fell back into place, covering his teeth, but he didn't stop growling.

"I hope you didn't teach him that, thinking you were clever," Paul, Jr., said.

"He's just got a thing," Tom said. "He thought you were threatening me."

"Well, I don't think it's funny," Paul, Jr., said.

"Neither do I, stupid," Tom said. "Just don't say anything about this to Mom or Dad."

"You think he really would have bitten me?" Paul, Jr., asked.

"I don't know," Tom said. "I'm glad we didn't have to find out."

"He scared me," Paul, Jr., said, "I'll tell you that. He really scared me."

Tom didn't know what to say.

"There's a box of dog biscuits in the garage," he said. "A great big one. Go get a couple of biscuits and give them to him, to make friends again."

The moment Precious saw the dog biscuits in Paul, Jr.'s hands, he became a great big friendly puppy again. He wagged his hindquarters, sat down, and handed Paul, Jr., his paw. There was nothing left of the ferocious animal of just a moment or two before.

But Tom was reminded of it by the way in which Precious ate the dog biscuits. They were the jumbo size, "for very large dogs," about eight inches long and nearly half an inch thick. Precious ate them like peanuts, his massive jaws effortlessly crushing them to powder.

Paul, Jr., couldn't keep his mouth shut about what had happened. He told their parents at dinner.

"You know what it may be," Dr. Lockwood said. "He may just be irritable because he's uncomfortable in the heat."

"What should we do, get him a haircut?" Tom asked.

"Why not?"

"Who ever heard of a dog with a haircut?" Tom countered.

"You ever see a French poodle?" his father replied, effectively shutting him up. "What we have here is a dog bred for English winters, with a coat to keep him warm in icy winds, and we've got him living in a semitropical climate. I don't see why the idea of a haircut is so absurd."

"Call me after school tomorrow, Tom," Mrs. Lockwood said. "I'll ask Dr. Harte about it when I'm at the university."

When he called, Mrs. Lockwood told Tom to take the dog to the College of Veterinary Medicine. Dr. Harte would examine him and probably see to having his hair cut.

At Dr. Harte's office, Tom quickly learned that the doctor was more interested in hearing Tom's version of the episodes of viciousness than in giving Precious a routine physical checkup.

Tom resisted the temptation to make excuses for Precious. He had been frightened by Precious's treatment of Paul, Jr., the day before, and by the earlier incidents. Dr. Harte heard him out.

"Can I talk to you about Precious without your repeating anything to your mother?" Dr. Harte asked.

"Yes, sir."

"I'm a little worried about Precious," Dr. Harte said. "Your mother brought in his pedigree for me to look at and asked me what I thought about it. I told her I thought there was a chance he was inbred. She didn't want to hear that, so I just shut up."

"I don't know what that means," Tom admitted.

"I wish your mother had come to me before she bought Precious," Dr. Harte said, "instead of afterward. I would not have sent her to the kennel where she bought him."

"Why not?"

"There are two kinds of people who raise dogs," Dr. Harte said. "One kind loves dogs and is happy to make a living doing something satisfying. The other kind loves money and raises dogs like a crop, trying to get the largest harvest for the least money."

"And you think the people who bred Precious are the second kind, right?" Tom asked.

"I hope I'm wrong," Dr. Harte said. "What sometimes happens, Tom, is that they inbreed."

"I still don't know what that means," Tom said.

"It means that they breed the dogs too close. Not brother to sister, because they couldn't get away with that, but cousin to cousin. When you do that, nature seems to pass on the worst characteristics, either anatomical or psychological, or both. You understand what I'm telling you?"

"I think so," Tom said. "Genetics?"

"It's all genetics. Dogs are bred, by good breeders, to improve the breed. You get a good bird dog and a good bird dog bitch and you mate them, and there's a pretty good chance that you'll get pups that are just as good as their parents, sometimes even better. But it works the other way, too. You get an overly nervous dog and you breed him, and you stand a good chance of getting overly nervous pups."

"Why would anybody want to do that?"

"For money," Dr. Harte said. "Some guy is in the dog breeding business, and one breed suddenly becomes very popular. He can sell all the dogs, Old English sheepdogs, for example, that he can get his hands on. Since what he's interested in is making money, not improving the breed, he mates dogs that shouldn't be mated. Pups all look very much the same when they're five, six, seven weeks old. So he won't have any trouble if he breeds a dog with, say, an anatomical flaw, weak hip joints or something like that. It won't develop in the pups until long after he's sold them."

"You think Precious has an anatomical flaw?"

"If anything is wrong with Precious, it's not anatomical. He's a beautiful animal, solidly muscled, in every way a very good physical specimen of his breed. I'm a little worried about his psychological state."

"You want to tell me why?"

"Whenever you inbreed dogs, you're going to come up with some pups that, when they mature, aren't quite right. A bird dog that won't hunt, for example. A Labrador that won't retrieve or go near the water. One that's just stupid. Conscientious dog breeders won't inbreed animals like that. Other people will."

"Whatever Precious is, he's not stupid," Tom said.

"Precious is an Old English sheepdog," Dr. Harte said. "Think what that means. For hundreds of years, his ancestors were bred to develop dogs that would protect sheep. That meant actually going out and driving away wild dogs and maybe even, centuries ago, wolves. Certainly foxes, wildcats, any other predators that would attack sheep. And, because shepherds work alone, the dogs became one-man dogs. I'll bet you a dime to a doughnut that Precious has picked out somebody in your family and decided he belongs to him."

"Me," Tom said.

"I thought so," Dr. Harte said. "Okay, so Precious doesn't have any sheep to protect. That shepherding instinct will probably be transferred to you, and he'll become a splendid watchdog."

"He has," Tom said.

"The problem with Precious is that he's likely to be too much of a good thing," Dr. Harte said. "He may start to protect you, and your house, from imaginary dangers. He may grow very jealous of somebody else—your mother, for example—who is giving you affection. He's liable to get into the habit of taking your side in a fight, as he did when you and your brother got into one."

"And what you're saying is that he could become dangerous."

"He weighs, as we just found out, one hundred three pounds," Dr. Harte said. "That's a lot of angry dog, Tom."

"What do we do about it?" Tom asked.

"You try to train him. You watch him. You hope."

"And if he still turns vicious?"

"Then you put him down, Tom," Dr. Harte said gently. "Before he hurts somebody."

"Are you telling me I should expect that?"

"I'm telling you that both sets of Precious's grandparents were cousins," Dr. Harte said. "Statistically, there is evidence that when that happens there is a high incidence of canine schizophrenia. Do you know what that means?"

"That means a split personality, doesn't it? Like Dr. Jekyll and Mr. Hyde?"

"Exactly. And from what my medical doctor friends tell me, canine schizophrenia is very much like the illness in humans. They also tell me it looks as if it's a lot easier to treat in humans."

"What you're really saying is that you think there's a possibility that Precious is crazy," Tom said.

"I didn't say that," Dr. Harte said. "I said you should watch him carefully for any signs that he's not quite normal. *If,* and I say *if,* we find something out of the ordinary, we can worry about it then."

Precious, who had been lying on the floor under the stainless-steel table in Dr. Harte's office through all this, suddenly grew bored. He got to his feet, leaped effortlessly onto the table, and gave Dr. Harte his paw.

There was nothing wrong with Precious, Tom decided,

watching him smooch Dr. Harte, except maybe he was too smart for his own good. He probably had figured out that he was big and could get away with more than a Dachshund could.

Dr. Harte shook Precious's paw and let go of it. Precious gave it to him again.

"He's obviously a splendid judge of character," Dr. Harte said, smiling, shaking the paw and scratching Precious's ears. "I don't think we have anything to worry about, Tom. I just thought I should mention what I did."

CHAPTER 9

WHEN THEY GOT TO THE SUBJECT OF Precious's haircut, Dr. Harte made Tom feel more than a little guilty.

"I thought you were more interested in his appearance than his comfort," Dr. Harte said. "Every time I see him, he looks as if he's been groomed to enter a dog show."

"I just don't like his hair to get matted," Tom said. "I've never even thought of entering him in a dog show."

"You could show him," Dr. Harte said. "Maybe you should. His body is perfect."

"He's a house dog," Tom said. "He's part of the family."

"In that case, we'll cut that fur coat off him," Dr. Harte said. "He won't be as beautiful, but he'll be a lot more comfortable."

It was clear to Tom that the veterinarian thought they'd finally decided to do what was best for Precious.

"There's no reason you can't clip him yourself," Dr. Harte said. "And he would probably like it better if you did the clipping rather than some stranger, but the first time I think you'd better see how an expert does it."

The expert turned out to be a girl, Ellen Watson, whom Dr. Harte introduced as one of his students. She was herself the daughter of a veterinarian and had been clipping dogs, she said, since she "got bored with the Brownies."

The first thing Ellen did was make friends with Precious, shaking his paw, scratching his ears and ribs, and giving him a dog biscuit.

83

"Whoever's been grooming him has done a good job," she said to Tom.

"I've been combing his hair," Tom said.

"Well, you've been doing it right," Ellen said. "Sometimes I see Old English sheepdogs whose hair is so matted I'd like to boil their owners in oil. What a lot of owners do is keep the outside fluffed up, so the dogs look good. The inside, close to the skin, gets matted and tangled, so that the hairs pull against each other, and it hurts the dog to walk across the floor."

Ellen Watson was a really nice person, Tom decided, and a nice girl. It was further proof of his theory that all the girls he liked were at least five years older than he was.

Ellen opened a cabinet door and took out a muzzle.

"You think he'll let me put this on him?" she asked. "Or do you think you'd better do it?"

"He's never worn a muzzle before," Tom said. "I'd better do it."

He took Precious by surprise. By the time Precious realized what was happening to him, the muzzle was on, and all he could do was try to push it off with his paw.

"Is this going to hurt him?" Tom asked.

"Not if we do it right," Ellen said. "But with a pooch that big, I don't like to take chances. I've grown used to having five fingers on each hand."

"What are you going to do when you clip his head?" Tom asked. "You can't clip it when he's wearing a muzzle."

"You don't clip their heads," Ellen explained. "That way they don't know they've been clipped."

"Huh?" Tom asked, confused.

"I'm glad you brought it up," Ellen said. "Listen, when we finish with him, he's going to look really weird. But, whatever you do, don't laugh at him. He's going to know that something has changed, and the last thing we want to do is make him feel ridiculous."

"You're trying to tell me he knows, he cares, what he looks like?"

"Absolutely," Ellen said. "And if he knows you're laughing at him, it will really bother him."

Tom decided Ellen was not putting him on.

"Okay, I won't laugh," he said.

"Remember that," she said. " 'Cause he really is going to look silly when we're finished with him."

Ellen took an electric clipper from a drawer. She showed Tom how it had to be lubricated before use.

"Watch the edge," she said, handing it to him. "It's not supposed to nick the skin, but if you're not careful, sometimes it does."

"I thought you were going to do it," Tom said.

"More psychology," Ellen said. "You start it, someplace easy. He'll decide that if you're doing it to him, then it can't be something terrible. And when he gets used to the buzzing and the sensation, I'll take over."

Ellen showed Tom where he was supposed to start cutting. He snapped the switch on. Precious looked curiously at the device in Tom's hands. Then, when Tom actually started cutting his coat along the top of his back, he stiffened and growled.

"It's all right, Precious," Ellen said.

"Shut up, dummy," Tom said. "I'm not going to hurt you."

The clippers were powerful and efficient. Long hanks of hair, as big as a hand, started falling onto the stainless-steel table. Tom made half a dozen cuts, and Precious, although his muscles were still tense, stopped growling.

"I'll take it now," Ellen said. "The way you're cutting, we'll be here all day."

He handed her the clippers and stood in front of Precious, scratching the dog's ears. Ellen went to work with the clippers.

Tom was really awed by her skill. Her movements were swift and sure, and so gentle that Tom decided Precious didn't know what was happening to him. He was far more concerned about the muzzle over his mouth than he was about the machine cutting his hair off.

It didn't take long at all to get the hair off of his back and sides, and from his legs. Ellen left the hair on his feet intact, and she left a ball of hair where his tail would have been if he had had a tail. Trimming the underside of him was more difficult, because Precious didn't like to lie on his back and kept trying to get back on his feet after Tom had rolled him over. The last part of his body to get clipped was his chest and shoulders. Finally, Ellen was finished.

"You can take off the muzzle now," she said.

Precious was visibly delighted to get rid of the muzzle. He shook his head and scratched his head. Then, curious, he sniffed at his body. He didn't seem to notice anything out of the ordinary. As if to thank Ellen for stopping whatever she had been doing, he handed her his paw.

Tom bit his lip. By any standard known to man, Precious was the most ridiculous-looking dog he had ever seen. Flowing hair concealed the features of his head and feet. The rest of him, despite his powerful muscles, looked like a skinny greyhound.

"He'll be a lot more comfortable now," Ellen said.

"How long will it take before it grows back?" Tom asked.

"Six months," she said. "By the time he needs his overcoat for the winter, he'll have it."

She handed him the telephone.

"What's this for?" he asked.

"Call your family and warn them about what you're bringing home," Ellen said. "And tell them not to laugh."

The whole family, including Barbara, who had arrived unannounced to welcome Paul, Jr., home from college, was waiting for Precious and Tom when they got back.

Mrs. Lockwood put her hand over her mouth.

Dr. Lockwood swore.

Paul, Jr., and Barbara bit their lips.

Precious ran from one to another, delighted to see them.

"Don't anyone laugh!" Tom said.

"That is the most absurd-looking dog I have ever seen," Dr. Lockwood announced. But he dropped to his knees and scratched Precious's back, high up by the shoulders, where Precious could not reach with his paws.

"He's going to be a lot more comfortable," Tom said. "And his coat will grow back by the time it's cold."

"We should have clipped him as soon as it got warm," Mrs. Lockwood said.

"I feel like a fool," Dr. Lockwood said. "We should have thought about it much sooner."

Precious was delighted to have the whole family assembled in one place, and to have the attention he was getting. He acted like an overgrown puppy. It was difficult to believe that the same dog, only the day before, would have leaped at Paul, Jr., if Tom hadn't held him back.

During dinner, Dr. Lockwood asked how much time Barbara had off from the newspaper.

"They owed me some overtime," she said. "I've got five days, including the weekend. And it doesn't count as vacation."

"Do you want to spend it here, or would you like to visit the French Quarter?" Dr. Lockwood asked.

The question had sort of flown in from outer space, and the rest of the family, as well as Barbara, looked at him in confusion.

"The French Quarter?" Paul, Jr., spoke up first. "As in New Orleans? *That* French Quarter?"

"That French Quarter," Dr. Lockwood said.

"You want us all to go to the French Quarter?" Mrs. Lockwood asked. Dr. Lockwood nodded. "It would cost a fortune," she said, dismissing the idea as another of her husband's familiar flights of fancy.

"I happen to know of an apartment we can use," Dr. Lockwood said, enjoying every moment of his family's confusion, "at a very good price. It would be a little crowded, because there are only two bedrooms, but the price is very attractive."

"How much exactly?" Mrs. Lockwood asked suspiciously.

"Free," Dr. Lockwood said, smiling.

"Free?" she asked. "Whose apartment is it?"

"The company's," he explained.

"And what's the company doing with an apartment in the French Quarter?"

"Spending a lot less money to put up salesmen and technicians than it did when they stayed in hotels," Dr. Lockwood said. "It was Colonel Switzer's idea, actually. He calls it 'logistic efficiency.'"

"How long has this been going on?" Paul, Jr., asked.

"Three, four months. We kept it sort of a secret, so that people wouldn't find things to do in New Orleans. But the idea is sound, it's saving us money, and there's not going to be anybody using it for the next week. Would you all like to go or not?"

Paul, Jr., drove the station wagon to New Orleans. His father sat beside him. Barbara and Mrs. Lockwood sat behind them. Tom and Precious rode in the rear-facing seat in the back.

Most of the time, they were on Interstate I-10, but there was a twenty-mile stretch in Mississippi where the interstate was not yet completed, and they had to go through several small cities.

Paul, Jr., was stopped by a red light. Precious, who had been sleeping, woke up, sat up, and looked around. Two young men in a Volkswagen were behind them. They had never before seen a dog looking like Precious, and they started laughing at him. Tom had been watching, and he realized they weren't being nasty. Precious was funny-looking. If he had been in the Volkswagen, he probably would have laughed, too.

The young man in the passenger seat rolled down his window and stuck his head out. He made a gesture for Tom to roll down his window. Tom cranked it down.

"Hey, what kind of a dog is that, any—" the young man asked. That was as far as he got. Precious threw himself furiously at the half-open window, trying frantically to force his body through the narrow opening.

"What the hell is going on back there?" Dr. Lockwood called, turning to look. The traffic light turned green, and Paul, Jr., started up. The sight of the funny-looking dog trying to claw his way through a half-opened window so startled the driver of the Volkswagen that he stalled the car. The Lockwood station wagon pulled away from him.

Precious, apparently believing that he had frightened the other car away, stopped trying to get through the window and permitted Tom to drag him inside.

"I asked what that was all about," Dr. Lockwood said.

"Precious didn't like the guy in the Volkswagen behind us," Tom explained. "He was laughing at him."

"Well, then," Dr. Lockwood said, chuckling, "good for Precious!"

For a moment, Tom was startled by his father's reaction to Precious's vicious behavior. The last thing he had expected was chuckling approval. Then he realized that his father hadn't understood what had happened, that he hadn't been paying much attention and thought that Precious had only barked at the car behind them.

After thinking it over for a moment, Tom decided that the best thing to do was nothing. If he told his father that Precious had been doing much more than barking, it was possible that Paul, Jr., would chime in that Precious had tried to attack him the day before.

And then, as if Paul, Jr., had been reading his mind, he called to Tom from the front seat: "Did it again, did he?"

"Yeah," Tom replied.

"Did what again?" Mrs. Lockwood asked.

"Private joke, Mom," Paul, Jr., said.

The apartment Wallwood Microtronics had rented was right in the center of the French Quarter, literally within a stone's throw of the cathedral on Jackson Square. A plaque on the outside of the building said that it had been built in 1828. It looked it, Tom thought, somewhat sourly. The building was old and dirty, and the large double doors leading from the street to the foyer looked as if they were about to collapse from age.

Once they were inside the building, however, Tom saw that it had been completely renovated. A beautiful antique crystal chandelier hung over the stairwell, and the stairs were thickly carpeted.

"I hate to think what this place costs the company," Dr. Lockwood said. "But that insane figure is cheaper than the really berserk prices they charge for hotel rooms in this town."

Precious explored the apartment, sniffing at the furniture and the carpet and the walls suspiciously, and then establishing himself on a couch facing the door.

"And where does a hundred-three-pound sheepdog lie down?" Dr. Lockwood asked.

"Anywhere he wants to," Paul, Jr., and Tom chorused. Precious sensed that he was the subject of the conversation, looked at his family, and then lay his head carefully on his paws again.

"I wish I could do that," Dr. Lockwood said. "Just drop off to sleep the way Precious does."

"Just because you can't see his eyes doesn't mean he's asleep," Tom said. "He's not asleep. He's preparing to defend us from the barbarians at the gate."

Dr. Lockwood chuckled. "We had to put a thousand-

"You know better than that," Paul, Jr., said. "That guy deserved what he got, but I don't want to try to explain that to a cop."

He was right, Tom realized. He grabbed Precious's leash, put his hand through the loop so that it was around his wrist, and started running down the alley.

Precious thought it was a new game and yipped happily.

dollar burglar alarm in here," he said. "What we really should have done was send Precious over. It would take a very courageous, or a very foolish, burglar to try to get past him."

"'Nice little doggy,' the burglar said," Tom quipped, "just before the doggy ate his right arm."

"Oh, don't talk like that. Precious wouldn't really bite anybody," Mrs. Lockwood said. "He's all bluff. All bark and no bite."

"The hell he is," Paul, Jr., said.

"Just because your father swears all the time," Mrs. Lockwood said, "doesn't mean that you have to, Paul."

"Sorry," Paul said.

"You and Tom take Precious for a walk," she said. "It was a long ride over here, and I'm sure he would like to inspect the local fireplugs."

Precious jumped off the couch the moment he saw Tom pick up his collar and leash. It wasn't that he wanted to inspect fireplugs, Tom realized. He didn't like this place. He wanted to go home.

They took him first to Jackson Square, where, barking at something he had never seen before, a flock of maybe two hundred pigeons, he caused a mass take-off of the birds. The pigeons swooped and soared over the statue of Andrew Jackson, finally landing across the street by the French Market coffeehouse. The streets were crowded with tourists and what Tom thought of as characters, young people (and some not so young) in strange clothes and hats.

Tom and Paul, Jr., got a lot of smiles from people who thought Precious was silly-looking, and even some cracks, some funny, some nasty:

"Could you give me the name of your pooch's barber?"

"What is that, the world's biggest lapdog?"

"Is that really a *dog*?"

One indignant elderly woman told Tom and Paul, Jr., they should be ashamed of themselves for "humiliating that poor animal that way."

Precious didn't seem to like much about New Orleans after they left Jackson Square. He walked between Tom and Paul, Jr., and, to Tom's surprise, didn't even pull at his leash.

Without knowing where they were going, they wandered around the French Quarter for more than an hour, looking at the shops and at the other tourists and what Paul, Jr., called the weirdos.

And then they met a weirdo in the narrow alley that runs between the Cathedral and the Calibado, one of New Orleans's oldest streets. The weirdo was about Paul, Jr.'s age. He wore a floppy-brimmed black hat, a sweatshirt, and farmer's overalls. His face was decorated with swirls of red and yellow and he carried an umbrella decorated about the same way.

He was spinning the umbrella as he sort of skipped down the alley toward Tom, Paul, Jr., and Precious.

And then he spotted Precious. "Wow!" he said. "What a far-out hound!"

Tom smiled. That was the third time someone had used those exact words to describe Precious's haircut.

"It's a ferocious lion from the jungle, that's what it is," the guy with the painted face said. "And I'm a famous lion tamer!"

He collapsed his umbrella and then waved it at Precious.

"Down, lion!" he said. "Down, lion!"

"Watch it, you damned fool!" Paul, Jr., said. Precious didn't think it was at all funny. He was growling.

"Growl, lion, growl!" the guy said, laughing.

He snapped the umbrella open in Precious's face. Precious, startled, backed up.

"Ha!" the guy said.

"Are you crazy?" Tom shouted. "Knock it off before—"

"Buzz off!" the guy with the painted face said nastily. "This is a ball!"

He collapsed the umbrella again, waved it like a sword in Precious's face, and then popped it open again.

Precious lunged, jerking his leash out of Paul, Jr.'s hand, knocking the umbrella out of the way, and sinking his teeth in the young man's arm.

"Oh, my God!" the young man howled, as Precious hung on.

Tom jumped on Precious's back, shouting "Bad dog! Bad dog!" and grabbed a handful of the thick hair on his head.

Precious, startled by what Tom was doing, let go of the young man's arm.

The young man, staring in disbelief at his ble[...] arm, crawled backward, away from them. Then he got [...] feet and ran down the alley in the direction he ha[...] from, holding his bitten arm with the other hand [...] ing in terror over his shoulder, afraid that the dog[...] away from Tom and chase after him.

Tom had pinned Precious to the cobble[...] alley with his body. Still holding him down, h[...] Paul, Jr., who was white-faced.

"Now what?" Tom asked.

"Now we get out of here, and take th[...] the apartment and keep him there."

"What about the guy he bit?"

"If he has any sense, he'll go se[...] said. He looked down at Tom. "Is it [...]

Tom let Precious go. Preciou[...] really angry with him, sat on his [...] his paw.

"Damn you, Precious!" To[...] offer his paw.

"Come on, come on," Pa[...] along."

"So what if one does[...]

CHAPTER 10

I T WAS TACITLY AGREED THAT TOM AND PAUL, Jr., would say nothing to their parents about Precious's having bitten the man who had teased him. There was no need to. Precious couldn't possibly have rabies. Dr. Harte had given him not only the rabies shot, but shots against every other canine disease he knew of.

Furthermore, the guy with the painted face had gotten what he deserved. That might not be a very kind thing to decide, but it was the truth. He had been teasing Precious, teasing him cruelly, for his own amusement, and Precious, scared, had defended himself. It wasn't as if Precious hadn't been minding his own business. The guy with the painted face had been looking for trouble, and he had found it.

Finally, if the cops got involved, it would be a real mess. Mrs. Lockwood would certainly have a fit, either against Precious or in defense of him. And that wouldn't change what had happened.

When his mother asked him if they had had a good time, Tom told her that Precious didn't really like New Orleans. She said that was understandable; he didn't know what city life was about, and all the people and noise made him uncomfortable.

At about five o'clock the doorbell rang. It was an unpleasant-sounding metallic buzzer, and it startled Precious. He leaped off the couch, growling and ready to defend his family.

95

Tom and Paul, Jr., exchanged looks. They were both convinced that it was the cops, that the young man Precious had bitten had gone to the police, and that it had taken the cops this long to find "a huge, weird-looking dog with all of his hair, except that on his head and feet, clipped."

"I wonder who that can be?" Mrs. Lockwood asked. She waited until Tom had put on Precious's collar and leash before opening the door.

It wasn't the cops; it was Colonel Switzer. He was in town, he said, to supervise the loading of some equipment onto a freighter bound for South America. He had heard the Lockwoods were going to use the apartment and decided to stop in and say hello.

Precious, overjoyed to see him, was wagging his entire hindquarters and whining to be freed from the leash.

"You can let him go," Mrs. Lockwood said. "He loves the colonel."

Precious was so glad to see the colonel, and so anxious to let the colonel know how much he liked him, that he went into the back room, picked up Barbara's purse in his mouth, and delivered it to the colonel, dropping it into his lap. When Barbara saw what he had done, she reclaimed her property furiously and shook her finger in Precious's face. Precious cringed before her reproof, so much that she felt sorry for him.

"He's really just a baby, Colonel," Mrs. Lockwood said. "As gentle as can be."

Tom looked at Paul, Jr., when she said that. Paul, Jr., shook his head.

For the rest of their time in New Orleans, Precious rarely left the apartment. He established himself on the couch by the door and just lay there. His appetite was off, and when they took him for a walk, they walked him away from the place where he'd had the run-in with the "lion tamer."

At last, they went home. Precious seemed not only happy to be there, but relieved. He didn't even seem very upset when Paul, Jr., and Barbara left. He seemed to understand that Paul, Jr., wasn't simply going for a ride, and he didn't even beg to be taken along. When Barbara got into her car, he didn't even go outside to see her off, and as soon as she'd gone, he walked into the living room and took up his position beside Dr. Lockwood's chair. Then he went to sleep.

"I think," Mrs. Lockwood said, putting Tom's thoughts into words, "that Precious is glad they're gone."

"So far as he's concerned," Dr. Lockwood said, "this is his mountain pasture, and we're his sheep. Not only did we bring other people into the pasture, we took him out of it. I think he's had all the excitement he wants for a while."

"He certainly didn't like New Orleans," Mrs. Lockwood said.

"He bit a guy in New Orleans," Tom blurted out. He had felt dishonest about keeping the story a secret.

"He did *what*?" Dr. Lockwood exclaimed.

Tom told them the story.

"That's terrible!" Mrs. Lockwood said when he had finished.

"Well, you can't say the man didn't deserve it," Dr. Lockwood said. "But a dog that bites—"

"He was defending himself," Mrs. Lockwood said, coming to Precious's defense. "That's different."

"What if it had been a child?" Dr. Lockwood said. "A child thinking he or she was playing with a dog, and Precious deciding he was being threatened and had to defend himself?"

"Don't be absurd," Mrs. Lockwood said. "Precious loves kids. You've seen that. This was a full-grown man who kept opening an umbrella in his face. If you had been there, you would have probably, oh, I don't know, broken the umbrella over his head."

"Yeah," Dr. Lockwood said. "If I had been there, I would have broken the umbrella over Precious's head. You simply can't let a dog get the idea that biting people is something he can get away with."

"Any dog, any animal, will bite if you get him into a corner," Mrs. Lockwood said.

Precious sensed that he was being talked about. He got to his feet, walked to Mrs. Lockwood, sat down, and handed her his paw.

"Look at him!" she said. "And then tell me he's vicious."

"The bottom line is that he's bitten two people," Dr. Lockwood said.

"*Two?*" Mrs. Lockwood asked.

"Me and the character in New Orleans."

"He hardly scratched you," she said. "Come on, Precious," she said, ending the argument. "We'll get you a bone to make up for what we did to you in New Orleans."

Precious, wagging his rear end, happily followed her out of the living room and into the kitchen.

In the next two months, Precious bit three people.

The first person he bit was Mr. Lopez at the shop. Everybody, including Mr. Lopez, agreed that it was Mr. Lopez's own fault.

Precious liked to sleep during the day, when Tom was at school, in the footwell under the computer keyboard desk. Everybody knew that, and they had come to think of the footwell as Precious's "cave." To his wife's annoyance, Mr. Lopez had formed the habit of scooting back and forth across the shop floor in his chair. The chair was mounted on small wheels, and Mr. Lopez had lubricated them with some newly developed super antifriction grease. Instead of standing up when he wanted to move from his desk to the workbench, or from the workbench to one of the computer terminals, he simply gave himself a shove and sailed across the room in his chair, "like a six-year-old in an amusement park," according to Mrs. Lopez.

It was understandable that Precious, who was sound asleep, was "startled and frightened" when Mr. Lopez came flying across the room in his chair one day, and brought himself to a stop with his foot. Precious's stomach was under the foot, and he took a nip at what was squeezing him.

"All he did was tear my trousers," Mr. Lopez reported. Tom knew that wasn't true, and that there were two-inch-long gashes in Mr. Lopez's ankle. But he agreed that what had happened was Mr. Lopez's fault and decided that Mr. Lopez was right to make as little of it as he could.

They even made a joke of it. Mr. Lopez got on the Telex and ordered a plastic sign from the plant.

CAUTION!
BEAR CAVE!
Do Not Disturb
Hibernating Beasts!

The sign was mounted just below the computer keyboard—in other words, just over the footwell.

Everybody knew that Precious had loved Mr. Lopez since he was a tiny puppy, and that he wouldn't have "nipped" him for the world unless he was frightened or hurt. There was absolute proof of this. In fact, for the next couple of days Precious nearly drove Mr. Lopez crazy with demonstrations of affection. He kept stealing Mrs. Lopez's purse and dropping it in Mr. Lopez's lap, and whenever Mr. Lopez leaned back in his chair and put his hands behind his head, as he habitually did when he was thinking, Precious lay his head in his lap, looked up at him with adoration, and waited to have his ears scratched.

Precious bit Mrs. Lockwood next.

That, too, was not Precious's fault. Precious was a

99

"walking garbage disposal" who would eat anything humans ate, including such things as cucumbers and radishes, which are not usually part of a dog's diet. He liked some foods better than others, of course, and at the top of his list of *really* good foods was liver of any kind, but preferably chicken liver.

From her college roommate, who was of German-Jewish extraction, Mrs. Lockwood had learned to make what she called "genuine Jewish chopped chicken livers," a bowl of which was her standard contribution to bridge party buffets and other social events of that nature. Making "genuine Jewish chopped chicken livers" involved sautéing the livers with onions in a skillet, and then running the sautéed livers and onions through a food processor with hard-boiled eggs and the necessary seasonings.

When Tom's mother was in the kitchen making the livers, Precious—aware that he would be permitted to lick the residue from the skillet and then from the food processor bowl—never moved more than three feet away from her. Just to make sure that Mrs. Lockwood realized he was there and that he was a very nice dog, worthy of chicken-liver remnants, Precious offered her his paw anytime he saw her looking in his direction.

What happened was that when Mrs. Lockwood bent over to give Precious the food processor bowl, Precious, still cleaning out the skillet, decided that she was trying to take the skillet away from him. He bit her on the hand.

The minute he bit her, he was sorry. He let go and ran out of the kitchen into the living room, where he hid behind Dr. Lockwood's chair. He lay on the carpet, watching the kitchen door for a long time. And then he spent most of the evening "making friends" with Mrs. Lockwood again. Precious was very appealing when he wanted to make amends, and he was forgiven for what he had done to her.

"Well, if you look at it calmly and honestly, it's as much

my fault as it was Precious's," Mrs. Lockwood said when it was all over and there was a bandage on the heel of her left hand, covering two teeth punctures. "I know how funny he is about his food, and I know how crazy he is about licking out the chicken-liver skillet. I should have 'engaged my brain,' as your father is always saying, and I didn't."

At first Tom was surprised that his father had very little to say about the latest "nipping" incident. But then he remembered that when his father was about to make a major decision, he said very little. Instead of talking, he was thinking—hard.

The third person Precious bit was Tom.

From the time he was small, Precious had chased along after Tom when he rode his bicycle. Mrs. Lockwood didn't like that. She was afraid that if Tom rode on the street, Precious would get run over by a car. As soon as she said that, Tom saw that she was right, and afterward, whenever he took Precious for a run, he rode his bike on the sidewalk. Precious quickly formed the habit of trotting along beside Tom, with his head near the rear axle of the bike.

At first, Tom rode slowly, but then he discovered Precious's ability to run alongside him at any speed that Tom cared to go. At most reasonable speeds, Precious didn't even seem to have to try to keep up. And Tom found out that even when he rode as fast as he could, he really couldn't get away from Precious. He could leave him behind for brief periods, for just as long as he could pedal his fastest. But the moment he ran out of breath and had to slow down, Precious caught up with him.

After the Mustang came along, of course, Tom rode his bicycle very little. Usually he did it when he wanted to give Precious exercise chasing after him. Or when the Mustang was in the garage for some reason, as it was on the day Precious bit him.

What Tom had planned to do was pick up the Mustang

at the Ford dealer's after school, go by the bus station to see what packages had come for the shop from the plant, and then take the packages to the shop. But when he went by the Ford garage, the car wasn't ready. So he rode his bike to the bus station, where he was delighted to find no packages. Then he went to the shop, told them what had happened, and was in turn told by his father that there really wasn't anything for him to do and that he should take Precious home, then go back to the Ford place and "stare mournfully at them until they finish the car."

Tom decided that it made no sense to go all the way home, drop Precious off, and then ride all the way back to the Ford place. He could reach the Ford place on side streets, and the exercise would do Precious good.

He was a block and a half from the Ford place. He was riding slowly, no hands, one moment; the next moment he was in the gutter. Precious was growling furiously and tearing at his ankle with his mouth. It took Tom a few seconds to realize that he'd dumped the bike somehow, he had no idea how. And it took him a few more to realize that Precious was biting him.

"Precious!" he shouted.

He couldn't shout very loud, because the fall had knocked the wind out of him, but he caught Precious's attention. First the dog stopped growling and sort of shaking Tom's ankle, and then he let go of the ankle and slinked out of the gutter onto a patch of grass between the gutter and the sidewalk.

"Damn you!" Tom said. Precious cringed.

Tom started to feel pain, not in his ankle, but on the heel of his hand, which he had apparently stuck out in front of him when he felt himself falling, and on his right knee. He looked at his hand and saw that it was scraped bloody, and that tiny pieces of gravel had been imbedded in his skin. Then he pulled up his trouser leg and saw that his knee was scraped, although the trousers weren't torn. Finally, he pushed down his left sock and saw the angry red gashes on his ankle. There were holes in his sock, but there didn't seem to be any holes in him. Precious's teeth, he thought, had just scraped his skin.

He tried to figure out what had happened. The first thing he thought was that Precious had been scared when he'd taken the fall and gone bananas. But then, when he examined the bike to see what damage he had done, he saw some of Precious's long white hair stuck in the links of the chain. Then he understood.

Precious had gotten his head and its flowing long white hair too close to the bike, and, as had often happened to Tom's trousers, the hair had been picked up by the chain and dragged into the drive gear.

That explained why the wreck had occurred, and it explained why Precious had bitten him. Not really *bitten* him, Tom corrected himself, but *nipped* at him, *scraping* his skin.

"Hey, I'm sorry," he said to the dog.

Precious, looking miserable, didn't move. He just lay where he had gone on the grass, with his head between his paws.

"I didn't mean to hurt you, dummy," Tom said. And then he chuckled. "Try to remember to keep your beard out of the machinery."

He stopped laughing when he stood up. His knee hurt. He had obviously bruised as well as scraped it. And he'd done a job on the rear gears of the bike, too, when he'd gone down.

There was nothing to do but push the bike to the Ford place. Precious tagged along after him, his head down so far that his nose almost touched the road. He was clearly a very unhappy dog, and Tom wondered if it was because he was sorry he had taken a nip at his boss or because he had been hurt when his hair had been pulled out by the roots after becoming meshed in the chain.

By the time he got to the Ford place Tom's ankle had

started to throb, and it felt wet. When he looked down at it, he saw that it was bleeding. The service manager saw it, too.

"What happened to you?" he asked.

"I fell off my bike," Tom replied.

"Let me see," the service manager said. "I'll put a Band-Aid on it for you." He took a ten-second look and announced that a Band-Aid wasn't going to do it. "If you think you can drive, go to your doctor. Or I'll take you. But that needs a doctor. It's a puncture wound, and they're dangerous. They infect right away."

Tom drove himself to the doctor's office. He left Precious in the car and hobbled inside. The nurse took about as long a look at his ankle as the Ford service manager had taken, before leading him into the first-aid room.

"What happened to you?" Dr. Sheldon asked. He was the family physician and more. He was one of Dr. Lockwood's cronies.

"I fell off my bike," Tom said.

Dr. Sheldon raised one eyebrow but said nothing. He cleaned and dressed the wounds on Tom's ankle, and then filled a hypodermic needle from a small glass bottle.

"What's that for?"

"Against tetanus and some other ambitious germs," he said. "I am presuming your bicycle has had its rabies shots?"

Tom flushed with embarrassment.

"Well, has he or hasn't he? Or wasn't it Precious who bit you?"

"It was Precious. I ran into him with my bike."

"A regular chip off the old blockhead, aren't you? You have to be careful around a dog that big. When they're excited, or hurt and excited, they can do a lot of damage."

"So I found out," Tom said. "Look, does Mom have to find out about this?"

"I won't lie about it," Dr. Sheldon said, after a few seconds. "But I don't have to volunteer any information, either, if that will make you happy. I can claim, if I'm caught, the confidentiality of the doctor-patient relationship. But you know how far that would get with your mother."

"She'd get all excited about the dog," Tom said.

"Yes," Dr. Sheldon agreed, "she would."

"No need for that," Tom said.

"Tom, you understand that you have a nasty puncture wound, but that it could easily have been a lot worse?"

"Yes, sir."

"Watch it with that dog," Dr. Sheldon said. "I mean it. Be really careful. I'm not saying he could kill you, but he could easily leave you scarred for life. You do understand that, don't you?"

"Yes, sir," Tom said. "I know."

CHAPTER 11

WHEN TOM CAME DOWNSTAIRS FOR BREAKfast the next morning, his ankle hurt. It was badly bruised—the skin around the bandages was blue-black—and when he moved it, he felt like it was being torn apart.

He limped into the downstairs bathroom and helped himself to a couple of aspirin. Then he limped into the kitchen and washed down the aspirin with his orange juice.

"Hurts, huh?" his father asked him.

"A little," Tom replied jokingly. "But you ought to see the other guy."

Tom was relieved that Dr. Lockwood didn't say anything further about the ankle.

"If you didn't go to school today," Dr. Lockwood said, "would that start an inexorable chain of events that would see you doomed to a life of manual labor?"

"You mean," Tom asked, laughing, "could I stay home and still pass?"

"I would hate to have you on my conscience," Dr. Lockwood said. "'If only his father had been more strict, Tom Lockwood could have done something with his life other than pick up trash along the highways.'"

"I could cut school," Tom said, "without flunking the year. But the ankle isn't really that bad. Just sore."

"I wasn't thinking about the ankle," Dr. Lockwood said. "I've got to go to New Orleans overnight, and I'd like some company."

"I accept," Tom said quickly. "What's going on?"

"Colonel Switzer, that jack of all trades, has come up with a guy, somebody he knew in the service, who may be just the man we need to send to the Tokyo office. There aren't too many American computer types who speak Japanese. Charley Walton wants me to talk to him."

"Won't I be in the way?"

"If you would be, I wouldn't have asked you to come along. The sacrifice required of you will be the wearing of a suit, complete with shirt and necktie. We're going to take him to dinner."

"I'm just happy," Tom replied, "that you realize how much of a sacrifice it is for me to give up school to go to New Orleans and eat an expensive dinner at a fancy restaurant."

"Well," his father said, "just gulp down your breakfast with your customary gluttony, pack your suit, and we'll go."

When he carried his suitcase out to the station wagon, Tom was surprised to see Precious in the backseat.

"Is he going?" Tom asked.

"Why not?" his father said. "Get in."

As soon as they got on the interstate highway, Dr. Lockwood stopped playing games.

"The reason I brought Precious along," he said, "is that I am fond of your mother."

"Sir?" Tom asked.

"I would hate to have Precious do to her what he did to you," Dr. Lockwood said.

Tom could think of nothing to say to that.

"To answer the question in your mind," Dr. Lockwood said, "Ed Sheldon thought it over and decided that his obligation to the family was stronger than his obligation to keep his word to you."

"It wasn't that bad a bite," Tom said lamely. "You want to know what happened?"

"Don't you think I have a right to know?" Tom's father said.

"He caught his fur in the chain," Tom said. "I dumped

the bike. It must have really hurt him. He was frightened—
and hurt."

"The point, Tom," Dr. Lockwood said, "is that dogs
aren't supposed to bite people, no matter what happens."

"There's such a thing as provocation," Tom said.

"Ed Sheldon said that you were very lucky," Dr.
Lockwood said. "Precious easily could have done some very
nasty permanent damage to your leg."

"But he didn't," Tom protested. "He didn't really hurt
me."

"I don't believe that," his father said. "I saw you wincing
with pain when you walked into the kitchen. That wasn't a
nip, Tom, that was a bite, a nasty bite, and one that very
easily could have been a whole lot worse."

"You're leading up to something," Tom said. "You want
to tell me what?"

"I'm stating the problem," his father said. "You can
never solve a problem unless you put it on the table and
shine bright lights on it. That's what I'm doing. Once you
understand the problem, then you can start to find a solution for it."

"Okay," Tom said. "The problem is that I hurt the dog,
and he hurt back. My stupidity."

"Come on," his father said. "You're avoiding the issue.
The problem is that we have an enormous dog who is
dangerous."

"Well," Tom said, aware that he had suddenly become
angry and was actually close to tears, "why don't we just get a
gun and shoot him, then?"

He was looking at his father as he spoke, and he knew
that what he was saying was making his father very angry.
Dr. Lockwood's face suddenly went white, and the skin
tensed. The last time he had said something fresh and angry
to his father, his father had slapped his face. That had happened not more than three or four times in Tom's memory,
and the thought of it was still painful.

His father controlled his temper now, however, although Tom could see that it took a good deal of effort.

"I brought you along," his father said, after a pause that lasted at least thirty seconds, "to talk this over with you as an adult. A young adult, maybe, but an adult. Not an emotional child."

"I'm sorry," Tom said. "I really am sorry."

"Yeah," his father said. "Me, too. Tom, the last thing in the world I want to do is kill Precious. But let's face it, son, that's one of our options. Maybe we won't have to select that option, and, God knows, I hope we don't have to. But it's one of the options, and there's no getting around that."

Precious, who had been asleep, heard his name mentioned, stood up on the backseat, and leaned forward and licked first Dr. Lockwood's ear and then Tom's.

"Oh, damn you, Precious," Dr. Lockwood said, and Tom saw that his father was having trouble controlling his emotions, too.

"Well," Tom asked, "what are we going to do with him?"

"Let's finish laying out the problem," Dr. Lockwood said. "First we admit that he bites people. That he's vicious. Then we ask ourselves, why is he vicious?"

"I don't know," Tom said. "I always thought that vicious dogs got that way because they were mistreated when they were puppies."

"Or bred to be vicious," Dr. Lockwood said. "Guard dogs, that sort of thing. Or bred *and* trained to be vicious."

"Well, nothing like that has happened to Precious."

"Yeah, that's what I concluded," Dr. Lockwood said. "But I have another idea. You want to hear it?"

"Please."

"You remember how young he was when we got him?"

"Five weeks."

"And your mother said that Precious's mother had rejected him?"

"I remember that."

"Maybe that had something to do with it," his father said.

"You think so?"

"I don't know," Dr. Lockwood said. "Canine psychology is another awesome gap in my knowledge. I guess what I'm leading to is that after I gave this problem a whole lot of thought, the only conclusion I could draw is that I don't know what to do about him because I'm working in ignorance."

Tom didn't reply.

"Tom, do you know the difference between ignorance and stupidity?" Dr. Lockwood asked.

Tom shook his head.

"Ignorance is not knowing," Dr. Lockwood said. "There's no shame in that. Stupidity is not doing whatever you have to do to find out what you need to know. That's shameful."

"I don't know what you're talking about," Tom confessed.

"Okay. Let me put it this way. I don't know why Precious is the way he is. If I don't know why he's the way he is, I obviously can't come up with any kind of solution. In that case, the thing to do is get the information I need. Seek out an expert, in other words, and put his knowledge to work."

"You're talking about Dr. Harte?"

"Right," Dr. Lockwood said. "I came to the conclusion that the only logical thing to do is lay the problem on Dr. Harte's desk."

"Yeah," Tom said.

"There is a problem connected with that, Tom," Dr. Lockwood said.

"What?"

"Worst possible scenario," Dr. Lockwood said, "which is that Dr. Harte will say there's something badly wrong, and permanently wrong, with Precious, and that the only way to handle the problem is to put him down."

110

"You think that's what's going to happen, don't you?" Tom asked.

"No, I don't," Dr. Lockwood said firmly. "But I am aware that it could happen. And if it does, I'll be prepared for it. And what this is all about, Tom, is preparing you for it, too."

"You didn't have to bring him along," Tom said, having a hard time talking. "Here we sit, with him listening, calmly talking about killing him."

"I really didn't think it was safe to leave him alone with your mother," Dr. Lockwood said. "And I guess I really wanted to have him along."

"Why?"

"I love that damned dog," Dr. Lockwood said. "That's what makes this so tough."

"Do you think Dr. Harte will be able to do something?" Tom asked. "Or is that just a last, desperate hope?"

"It's a last, desperate hope, Tom," Dr. Lockwood said.

The red lamp on the telephone-answering device in the apartment was flashing when they got there, and when Tom replayed the incoming message tape, Colonel Switzer's happy voice reported that he and Colonel Cliff Walker were in the bar of the Royal Orleans Hotel and would welcome the presence of Dr. Lockwood.

"I suspect that the colonels have been at the cheering cup," Dr. Lockwood said. "So I'd better get over there before our colonel hires the other one as chairman of the board. Can you amuse yourself for a couple of hours?"

"Sure."

"We'll go out for dinner at half-past seven, or maybe a little later. You be dressed and ready by then, okay?"

"Right."

After his father had gone to join Colonel Switzer, Tom took Precious for a quick walk, on side streets, and then went back to the apartment and watched television. He had been on the couch no more than two minutes when Precious, with remarkable grace and gentleness for so large a

111

dog, leaped up on the couch and laid his head in Tom's lap and went to sleep.

"The world's biggest lapdog," Tom said. Tears ran down his cheeks.

Dr. Lockwood telephoned at half-past seven and said that Colonel Switzer had made reservations for them at the Versailles restaurant, and that they were about to leave the Royal Orleans in a cab. They would stop by the apartment and pick him up. He was to be waiting on the curb.

Tom dressed quickly and, while he did, had what he thought was a mature thought. It was possible that his father would bring the colonel and the man he had with him back to the apartment. In case that did happen, it would be better to be careful about Precious. Tom took Precious, who went sadly and reluctantly, having sensed that he was about to be left, into the rear bedroom. He gave him food, water, two dog biscuits, and a chew toy. Then he closed the door on him and went outside to meet the taxi.

The man Colonel Switzer had brought for Dr. Lockwood to meet was very much like Colonel Switzer. Tall, heavyset, ruddy-faced, and pleasant. Both of them acted and looked like senior officers, Tom thought. He could easily picture them in uniform.

"I'm glad you're here, Tom," Colonel Switzer said, shaking his hand. "These two have already started talking in electronics gobbledygook, and I was beginning to feel like a dummy. You and I can talk."

And that's exactly what happened. Dr. Lockwood and Colonel Cliff Walker (retired) made small talk in the taxi on the way to the restaurant, which was on St. Charles Avenue, some distance from the French Quarter. But the minute they sat down at the table, they started talking about computers and the electronics that made them possible. So far as Tom and Colonel Switzer were concerned, they could have been talking in Latin or Apache. As a result, there were two very different conversations at dinner.

The food was superb, and Colonel Switzer surprised Tom by being able to tell him all about it. He said that he had been assigned mess duty when he was a young lieutenant and had been cooking as a hobby ever since. Before the meal was over, he had the chef sitting at their table, talking about his technique for making the crawfish bisque with which the meal had begun.

"What we'll do now," Dr. Lockwood said, after they had finished dinner and were standing on the sidewalk outside waiting for a taxi, "is go by the apartment and have a nightcap or two. But that poses a problem. We have a dog that sometimes doesn't like people. When we get to the apartment, Tom, you run ahead and lock him in the back room."

"I already did," Tom said.

"Good thinking," his father replied. Tom sort of beamed. "Then there's no problem."

"There's not a dog alive that doesn't like me," Colonel Walker said.

"You haven't met Precious," Colonel Switzer said.

"*Precious?*" Colonel Walker asked. "What is it, a ferocious Pekingese?"

"No, Cliff," Colonel Switzer said. "It's a hundred-twenty-pound Old English sheepdog. Big enough to be dangerous."

"I repeat, there is no dog in the world who doesn't adore me at first sight," Colonel Walker replied.

"Well, you better play it cool with this one," Colonel Switzer said. "Or learn how to play the piano with one hand. This dog can be bad news, Cliff. I'm not kidding."

"Okay. I won't mess with Precious," Colonel Walker said.

When they opened the apartment door, Precious growled deep in his throat and pawed angrily at the bedroom door. Even Colonel Walker was impressed.

"Now *that's* what I call a first-class burglar-scarer," he said.

"Shut up, Precious," Tom called. "It's us."

Precious shut up immediately and was silent for about five minutes, long enough for Dr. Lockwood to make drinks for everybody.

Then Precious started to whine.

"Shut up, Precious," Dr. Lockwood ordered.

"He just wants to come out and join the party," Colonel Walker said. "He can't understand why he's locked up."

"He's better off where he is," Dr. Lockwood said. "Has he got something to eat, Tom?"

"And drink, and a chew toy. And he had some dog biscuits."

"Well, take him this," Dr. Lockwood said, handing Tom a small bundle wrapped in aluminum foil.

"What's this?" Tom asked.

"A doggie bag from the restaurant," his father said. "For the doggie. It should shut him up."

Tom took the package from his father and started for the back room.

"Where are you going, Cliff?" he heard Colonel Switzer asking behind him, concern in his voice.

"To the gentlemen's rest facility," Colonel Walker replied.

"Stay away from that dog, Cliff," Colonel Switzer said sharply.

"I heard you, I heard you," Colonel Walker replied.

Tom waited until Colonel Walker went into the bathroom and closed the door before he opened the door to the rear bedroom. He stepped inside quickly and closed the door behind him.

Precious was beside himself with joy at seeing Tom. He was not even very interested in the doggie bag. Tom dropped to his knees in front of him, unwrapped the foil, and fed him the table scraps. Precious wolfed down the meat pieces and had just taken the bone from the prime rib of beef Dr. Lockwood had eaten when the door opened behind him.

114

Precious started to growl.

"Precious, sit!" Tom ordered.

"What do you say, Precious?" Colonel Walker asked, waving his hand at Precious.

Precious dropped the rib he had in his mouth. He sprang into the air, knocking Tom over onto his back.

Colonel Walker swore.

"Precious!" Tom heard his father shout. "Oh, damn you, Precious!"

Tom rolled over. He saw Colonel Walker. He was holding his face. There was blood, lots of it, oozing out between his fingers. Precious, growling furiously, was crouched, ready to jump at him again.

Tom leaped on the dog and knocked him down, pinning him to the carpet.

"Damn you, Cliff," Colonel Switzer said angrily. "I *told* you to leave that damned dog alone!"

"My God," Colonel Walker said, "that animal is crazy."

Dr. Lockwood and Colonel Switzer took Colonel Walker into the front room and closed the door. Tom saw blood on the carpet.

He let Precious go. Precious sat up. He gave Tom his paw.

"Are you all right with him, Tom?" his father called from the front room.

"Yeah," Tom called back.

When Tom didn't take Precious's paw, Precious stood up and walked over and licked his face.

"You just committed suicide, dummy," Tom said, wrapping his arms around Precious's neck.

CHAPTER 12

COLONEL WALKER REACTED LIKE AN OFFICER and a gentleman to being bitten by Precious after he had been warned to stay away from him.

He didn't want to go to the emergency ward of the hospital at all, because that would make the biting "official" and embarrassing to the Lockwoods. But he finally gave in when Colonel Switzer told him firmly that he had a choice "between medical attention and a two-piece ear."

At first they had trouble getting attention in emergency, which was jammed with people. Only a few of them seemed to be injured or really sick, and Tom was confused until he overheard Colonel Switzer say to his father, "These are the poor, who have no family doctor and come to the emergency ward for all their medical treatment."

"What are we going to do?" Dr. Lockwood asked.

"We have a real emergency. I'll get somebody to take care of Walker."

He disappeared into an elevator and was back in five minutes with a doctor and a nurse. The doctor took one look at Colonel Walker's ear and swore.

"That's a really nasty slashing bite," the doctor said.

"I cut myself shaving," Colonel Walker said.

"That's an animal bite," the doctor said. "You're lucky you didn't lose half your ear."

"I didn't come here to argue with you, Doctor," Colonel Walker said. "I want you to sew up my ear."

"I'll take care of your ear, but I'll have to make a report," the doctor said.

116

"You can make all the reports you want," Colonel Walker said. "Just so long as you quote me correctly as saying I cut myself shaving."

The doctor didn't argue with him. He cleaned and sutured the torn ear and then bandaged it.

"I heard somebody call you colonel," the doctor said.

"Signal Corps, retired," Colonel Walker said.

"Family pet, was it, Colonel?" the doctor asked.

Colonel Walker looked at him and said nothing.

"To tell you the truth, if you don't want to make a report, there's no way I can force you to," the doctor said.

"I had that feeling," Colonel Walker said.

"And I presume you know what the treatment is for a rabid animal bite?"

"A series of painful injections into the stomach wall," Colonel Walker said.

"Against the very good chance of a painful death," the doctor said.

"There are no rabies involved here," Colonel Walker said. "I'm not that much of a fool."

The doctor nodded.

"I'll tell you the kind of fool I am, Doctor," Colonel Walker said. "Sometimes I drink too much. And until very recently, I believed all dogs loved me on sight."

"And this one didn't?"

"The *razor with which I cut myself,* Doctor," Colonel Walker said, "apparently believed I posed a threat to my friend here." He laid his hand on Tom's shoulder. "If you need a guilty party, I'm he."

"Okay," the doctor said. "Go see your doctor in a couple of days—three, maybe—and have the sutures removed." And then he turned to face Tom. "And you, young man, had better buy a muzzle for your 'razor.'"

Tom nodded. He fought the tears that came into his eyes. Buying Precious a muzzle wasn't going to solve this problem. Precious hadn't bitten Colonel Walker because he thought the colonel was going to hurt Tom. He had bitten Colonel Walker because he was a vicious animal. And that meant he would have to be "put down," which was a polite way of saying that he would have to be killed.

On the curb outside the hospital, waiting for a taxi, Colonel Walker touched Dr. Lockwood's arm. "Consider my application for employment withdrawn," he said.

"I don't understand," Dr. Lockwood said.

"Even if you wanted to hire me after seeing my ability to make a fool of myself, I wouldn't want to get the job because your dog nipped me."

"He didn't nip you, Colonel," Dr. Lockwood said. "He bit you because he's a vicious animal. And that has nothing to do with whether or not you could do Wallwood Microtronics a good job in Tokyo. Charley Walton wants you, Colonel Switzer wants you, and so do I."

"Well, thank you."

"And if I were you, I think I'd sue me for what happened."

"You didn't bite me," Colonel Walker said, laughing.

"My dog did, and I'm responsible for my dog," Dr. Lockwood said.

"It wasn't the dog's fault," Colonel Walker said.

"You and I both know better than that, Colonel," Dr. Lockwood said. "And, for that matter, so does Tom."

"I wouldn't want you to put that animal down because of what happened to me."

"What happened to you, Colonel," Dr. Lockwood said, "was just the last, and the worst, incident in a series of unprovoked attacks."

"Then I'm really sorry," Colonel Walker said.

Precious seemed to sense that he was in deep trouble. When Tom and Dr. Lockwood got back to the apartment, he didn't even bark. He greeted them by approaching them slowly, sitting down, and offering his paw.

And that night he slept with Tom. When Tom woke up in the morning, Precious had his head on the pillow beside him.

Neither Dr. Lockwood nor Tom had any appetite in the morning, so they got into the station wagon and headed for home without breakfast. Two hours down the interstate highway, Dr. Lockwood turned off and stopped at a Mc-Donald's. He and Tom each ate two Egg McMuffins and drank two half-pints of milk. Then they ordered two Jumbo Burgers without lettuce or tomato and took them out to the car for Precious.

The condemned man, Tom thought, gets a hearty meal.

When they got home, they drove directly to the university. Precious dutifully followed them into the Veterinary Medicine building and up the stairs to Dr. Harte's office. Dr. Harte was teaching a class, and they had to wait more than an hour for him.

Then he walked through the door. "Well," Dr. Harte said. "Look who came to see me! Hey, Precious, how's my favorite lapdog?"

Precious ran to him and nuzzled him, giving him his paw.

"Precious is crazy, Dr. Harte," Dr. Lockwood said, his voice choked. "We came to ask you to . . . put him down."

Dr. Harte, who had dropped to his knees so he could scratch Precious's ears, looked at Dr. Lockwood.

"I thought something was wrong," he said. "Come on into the office."

Dr. Harte had his secretary bring them all coffee. Tom normally didn't drink coffee, but now it seemed easier to take it than to politely refuse and be offered milk or a Coke. He wanted to get this over with as quickly as possible.

Dr. Harte, however, was in no hurry at all. Even though he knew a lot of it from Tom's previous visit, he drew out from them the whole story, from the first time Precious

119

had taken a nip at somebody through the latest incident.

"Is that all?" he asked finally.

Tom and his father nodded.

"Well, I agree with Tom," Dr. Harte said, "that the bike incident could have happened to any dog. Precious was hurt and frightened, and when they're hurt and frightened, dogs bite. They are animals, after all, not little people who can't talk."

Neither Tom nor his father said anything in reply.

"The other incidents, and especially what happened last night, seem to make it pretty clear that something has to be done. That dog is powerful enough to kill somebody."

"I've never—" Dr. Lockwood said, and then stopped before going on. "Had a dog put down before. I don't know anything about it."

"But you are determined to put him down?" Dr. Harte asked.

"There is no other option, is there?"

"Yes, there is," Dr. Harte said. "It's not cheap, and—"

Dr. Lockwood waved his hand in a sign that meant money wasn't a problem.

"There's no guarantee of success," Dr. Harte went on.

"What is it?" Dr. Lockwood asked impatiently.

"Well, let's talk about what's wrong with Precious," Dr. Harte said. "For one thing, there's nothing physically wrong with him. He's really a nearly perfect example of a well-developed, highly intelligent, healthy, well-nurtured Old English sheepdog. The only thing wrong with him is that he's vicious. So why is he vicious? Certainly not because he was abused, or tormented, as a puppy."

"His mother rejected him," Tom said.

"That happens to pups all the time, Tom," Dr. Harte said. "And they grow up to be perfectly natural, unvicious dogs. I think, as I told Tom some time ago, Paul, that Precious is schizophrenic."

120

"Schizophrenic? Dual personality?" Dr. Lockwood asked. "Just like Dr. Jekyll and Mr. Hyde?"

"Tom asked the same question," Dr. Harte said, chuckling. "Yes. Just like Dr. Jekyll and Mr. Hyde."

"Phrased somewhat cruelly," Dr. Lockwood said, "you're saying Precious is crazy."

"That he is mentally unbalanced. Okay, crazy," Dr. Harte said.

"So what do you do with a crazy dog?" Dr. Lockwood asked.

"You try to guess what has unbalanced him," Dr. Harte said. "Since we know that he wasn't abused, that leaves only a physical defect."

"You mean he was born crazy?" Dr. Lockwood asked.

"Well, we can see from his pedigree that he's inbred. Some dirty word of a money-hungry breeder chose to produce as many puppies for sale as he could, as cheaply as he could. The result of inbreeding is well known: It more often than not passes on to the next generation the weakness of both father and mother. In this case, the weakness, the bad genetic trait, passed on wasn't physical. It was psychological."

"You're beginning to lose me," Dr. Lockwood said.

"Look at it this way," Dr. Harte said. "Every dog has to make decisions. There is a time to bite and a time not to bite. A dog who wouldn't bite under any circumstances would be as sick as Precious is. They have to make the decision that now I *can* bite, or fight, which is really what we're talking about, and now I *can't*. Precious doesn't have the ability to make that decision wisely."

"When is it okay?" Dr. Lockwood asked.

"Precious is an Old English *sheepdog*," Dr. Harte said. "As I once explained to Tom, his ancestors were bred to protect sheep, which means to fight any animal that poses a danger to the herd and to threaten the sheep by growling and pretending to bite them, without ever hurting any of them. That's asking quite a bit of a dumb animal."

"Where does this leave us with Precious?" Dr. Lockwood asked.

"When he bit the colonel last night," Dr. Harte said, "he was protecting Tom."

"Tom didn't need protection."

"That's the decision Precious is unable to make wisely," Dr. Harte said. "Without sufficient provocation, he did what he was bred to do. He protected his sheep."

"Well, what do we do about it?" Dr. Lockwood said.

"We can try to gentle him," Dr. Harte said. "You'll notice I said *try* to gentle him."

"How?"

"You could say that part of Precious's problem is that he's a male," Dr. Harte said.

"Oh, come on," Dr. Lockwood replied.

"I'm perfectly serious. The male dog is far more the aggressor than the female. Most females will fight only to protect their young. Males like it. So what we could try with Precious, if you're willing to pay the money and take the chance, is to take his masculinity away from him."

"Castrate him? Is that what you're talking about?"

"Yes. That often works, and in recent years, some of my colleagues and I have noticed something else that we find interesting, even if we can't explain it."

"What's that?"

"Dogs with aggressive personalities who have been anesthetized for surgery, and I mean for surgery besides a neutering operation, sometimes come out of the anesthesia gentled."

"Is that so? I wonder why."

"Nobody knows," Dr. Harte said. "And it doesn't happen all the time. But there's a chance that it would tend to gentle Precious. And there's another chance, a better

122

It wasn't until Tom went to bed that Precious forgave him. First he scratched at Tom's door, and then, when he was let in, he slowly and carefully crawled onto the bed. Tom didn't have the heart to make him get off, especially after Precious snuggled up next to him and licked his ear.

chance, that the neutering operation would gentle him."

"You're saying he can be cured?" Dr. Lockwood asked.

"I didn't say that, Paul. I said there's a chance," Dr. Harte said.

"Well, Precious certainly gets any chance we can give him," Dr. Lockwood said. "Let's do it."

"Yeah," Dr. Harte said. "Let's do it. Precious is too good a dog to throw away like a candy wrapper."

"When would you like to do it?"

"Right now," Dr. Harte said. "I've got an operating room scheduled for a class. What's the point in being head of your department if you can't get a little special treatment for your friends?"

"Thank you, Doctor," Dr. Lockwood said.

"I'll call you at home when we've finished with him," Dr. Harte said. "And you can plan on taking him home on Tuesday or Wednesday."

"Thank you," Dr. Lockwood said again.

"Yeah, thank you," Tom said.

"Come on, Precious," Dr. Harte said. "Let's take a little walk."

Precious, who had been lying on the floor in front of Dr. Harte's desk, got to his feet, looked at Tom and Dr. Lockwood, and then cheerfully followed Dr. Harte out of the room.

Tom looked at his father.

"He's got a chance," Dr. Lockwood said. "At least that."

"I feel a whole lot better now than I did when I walked in here," Tom said.

"Me, too," Dr. Lockwood said. "Now let's go home and gently break the news to your mother."

The telephone rang at a quarter to six. Tom grabbed it first.

"My name is Ellen Watson," the caller said. "May I please speak with Dr. Lockwood."

"One moment, please," Mrs. Lockwood said. She was on the kitchen extension.

"This is Tom Lockwood," Tom said.

"Oh, hi," Ellen Watson said. "I can talk to you. Dr. Harte asked me to call to tell you that Precious had the operation and just came out of the anesthesia."

"How is he?" Tom asked.

"Dopey, and sore," Ellen Watson said. "I just left him. But he'll be all right."

"Can I come see him?"

"I don't think that's a very good idea," Ellen Watson said. "If he sees you, he'll want to come home. We don't want him jumping around or getting excited for a couple of days. I'll call you every day, if you like, and let you know how he is."

"What about bringing him a chew toy or something?"

"It wouldn't hurt," she said. "Drop it off at Dr. Harte's office and I'll pick it up there."

"Thanks a lot," Tom said.

"My pleasure," she said. "It's not very professional, I suppose, but I really like that hound of yours. It would have been a shame to have put him down."

"You know it!" Tom said.

They had to wait until Wednesday to pick up Precious. Ellen Watson called on Tuesday and reported that during the night, Precious had somehow worked his muzzle off, and then pulled off the bandage over his abdomen. Before they caught him, he had pulled out half of his sutures, too. He hadn't opened the wound, but they thought it best to keep him another twenty-four hours.

When Tom got to the university after school on Wednesday, he found his father and mother waiting for him in the lobby. They went together to the small animal hospital. Dr. Harte was waiting for them there.

An attendant was sent for Precious. When he was led out, he seemed strange, and he was wearing a muzzle. His

hair around his stomach and hindquarters had been shaved and he was wrapped in wide adhesive tape.

"What's that for?" Mrs. Lockwood asked, as she dropped to her knees to scratch Precious's ears.

"Well, that protects the opening we had to make," Dr. Harte said.

"I meant the muzzle," she said.

"That's to keep him from tearing the bandage off," Dr. Harte replied, "and to keep him from eating the attendan⸺ Then he saw the look on her face. "I suppose that was i⸺ taste, but we always muzzle large dogs who are ⸺ They're frightened, and frightened animals bite."

"I thought this operation was going to sto⸺ doing that," she said.

"We hope it will. But the real reason for ⸺ keep him from tearing off the bandage."

What was really strange about Pre⸺ didn't seem to be glad to see any of them⸺ waiting for something to happen.

When they got back outside th⸺ Tom's Mustang and waited patien⸺ the front seat carefully, as if⸺ curled up.

When they got home, h⸺ carefully as he'd gotten in⸺ living room. He lay dow⸺ Lockwood's chair.

"I think he's in p⸺

"I think he's ju⸺ said. "He's sulkin⸺

"Don't be s⸺

"This on⸺

Tom w⸺ noon and ⸺ when it w⸺

CHAPTER 13

PRECIOUS WAS OBVIOUSLY "NOT HIMSELF" FOR the next several days. Tom really felt sorry for him. From the way he walked, it was evident that he was uncomfortable, if not actually in pain. But he refused to just lie in one place. He insisted on waiting under the breakfast table until the Lockwoods had finished their breakfast, as he always did, and then, when it was time, offering his paw for the habitual treat of toast remnants and plates to lick. And, whenever Tom and then Dr. Lockwood left for school and work, he walked slowly to the window in the living room and watched until they disappeared from sight.

To keep him from tearing at the bandage with his teeth, he had to wear a muzzle. He made it clear to everybody that not only did he hate the muzzle, but he also wondered what he had done to be forced to wear it. And he wondered why he was being punished by not being permitted to go to the shop with Dr. Lockwood or in the station wagon with Mrs. Lockwood when she shopped.

When any of the Lockwoods sat down for a moment, they could expect to have Precious's head suddenly laid in their lap, or to feel Precious's paw gently pushing at them. "Here I am," he seemed to be saying. "I don't know what I've done wrong, but it's all right. Punish me. I don't mind."

"I wish to hell he was that apologetic about taking bites out of people," Dr. Lockwood said at the supper table.

"He doesn't understand that biting people is a no-no," Tom said. "You heard what Dr. Harte said."

"That's all over now," Mrs. Lockwood said. "We've had that fixed."

Tom and his father exchanged glances. Dr. Harte had been careful to offer no guarantee, or even a lot of hope. He had made it perfectly clear that all the operation had done was give Precious another chance.

Mrs. Lockwood met Dr. Harte on the campus and asked him about removing the sutures in Precious's abdomen. He told her to have Tom bring him to the small animal hospital the next day after school, and she relayed the message to Tom that night.

Tom was standing in the kitchen drinking a glass of milk the next afternoon when the front doorbell rang. Precious growled, as he always did when the doorbell rang. Tom wondered if the growl was less ferocious than usual or if that was just wishful thinking on his part. Precious started for the front door, and Tom walked after him. He didn't think Precious posed any threat to anybody with a muzzle on, and as sore as he was.

Mrs. Lockwood beat Tom to the front door. She was obviously confused by the presence of an attractive young woman who had just asked her, "How's our patient?"

"Here he comes, Ellen," Tom called. "See for yourself."

Precious greeted Ellen Watson with a good deal of enthusiasm, shaking his rear end and trying to jump up on her to lick her face. Ellen dropped to her knees to keep him from jumping up.

"Mother, this is Ellen Watson," Tom explained.

"I suppose I should have called," Ellen said, "but time got away from me."

"Tom was just about to take Precious to the clinic to have his stitches taken out," Mrs. Lockwood said to Ellen, after Precious had calmed down enough to permit conversation.

"I know," Ellen said. "Dr. Harte told me. That's why I'm here. I thought it would be easier on Precious if I took them

128

out here. He's nobody's dummy, and he associates the small animal hospital with pain and confusion. I thought he might give Tom trouble getting him back inside."

"Oh, that's right," Mrs. Lockwood said. "You're one of Dr. Harte's students, aren't you?"

"That's right," Ellen said.

"Hey, that's nice of you, Ellen," Tom said. "Thanks."

"Do you know how to remove the stitches?" Mrs. Lockwood asked doubtfully.

"I put them in," Ellen said with a smile. "I feel responsible for them."

"Then you're a veterinarian?" Mrs. Lockwood asked.

"I got my degree last year," Ellen said, "and I've stayed on as a teaching assistant. I did the procedure—the operation—on Precious, while Dr. Harte explained what I was doing to one of his classes."

"Then I really should be calling you doctor, shouldn't I?" Mrs. Lockwood asked.

"I wish you'd call me Ellen," she said. "Where can I work on Precious? It won't be messy. What I need is something like a kitchen table."

"By a strange coincidence," Tom said, "we have a kitchen table. We keep it in the kitchen."

Mrs. Lockwood helped by clearing the kitchen table, but then she started to leave the room.

"I can't watch things like that," she said.

"Well, then, let me warn you about Precious," Ellen said. "What I'm going to do now is remove that wraparound bandage, which I'm sure is uncomfortable for Precious. And then the sutures in the wall of his abdomen. The sutures inside are self-dissolving. Then I'm going to put a super Band-Aid over the wound. We'll keep the muzzle on him for another three days, and then take it off. Knowing Precious as I do, I think he'll have the Band-Aids off five minutes after the muzzle comes off."

"Will that be all right?" Mrs. Lockwood asked.

"What I'm trying to explain is that he will have an angry-looking scar. He'll lick it. Let him. It may even suppurate a little. There's nothing to worry about unless he tears the wound open, and I think he's too smart to do that. If he does, of course, call me right away."

It took all of Tom's strength to pick up Precious. It wasn't only that he weighed one hundred twenty pounds; it was also that Precious didn't like to be picked up and, furthermore, sensed that something was going to happen to him. Tom had to pick up one hundred twenty pounds of stiff, reluctant, growling dog.

Ellen Watson scratched his ears once he was on the kitchen table, and gradually he stopped growling and relaxed his stiff muscles. Then he tried to smooch Ellen and offered her his paw. Finally, they were able to get him to lie down and then roll over on his side, where Ellen could get at the bandage.

"I'm going to hold down his hindquarters," she said, "and jerk the bandage off, while you hold down his shoulders and head. Use all your strength, because I want to get the sutures out while he's still on his side."

Precious struggled violently when the bandage was jerked off, taking some of his hair with it. But Tom was surprised that he didn't growl or even try to bite through the muzzle. Instead, he cried.

"When he does that," Ellen said as she removed the sutures, "I almost wish he'd try to bite. The one thing wrong with being a vet is that you can't explain to the patient what you're trying to do for him."

Tom was very impressed with the speed and obvious skill with which Ellen removed the sutures. It took her only several minutes to get them all out and to place a new dressing, which really did look like a super Band-Aid, over the wound.

"Okay," she ordered. "Now, don't let him go. I'm going

to grab his hindquarters, and together you and I are going to set him back on the floor. I want to get him off the table before he starts jumping around."

Together, they lowered Precious to the floor and let him go. The first thing he did was growl.

"That's just to let us know"—Ellen laughed, unafraid— "that he doesn't approve of what we did to him."

Then he got quickly, awkwardly to his feet and sniffed at the dressings. And then, as if he suddenly realized he had a chance to get away from his tormentors, he made a dash for the living room. Ellen laughed again.

"If humans weren't so concerned with appearances," she said, "they'd run away from their doctors in exactly the same way."

Precious came back into the room before Ellen and Tom had finished cleaning up the table and replacing the table-cloth and other things that had been removed from it. He went to Ellen and gave her his paw.

"He forgives you," Tom said, chuckling.

"That proves he's a very nice pooch," Ellen said. "If someone had knocked me over on my side, held me down, jerked a bandage off my belly, and then used shiny and painful tools on it, I would take a whole lot longer to forgive her."

Ellen's prophecy that Precious would have the super Band-Aid off his abdomen five minutes after they removed his muzzle came true. And then he started to lick the scar, as she had said he would.

But that seemed to mark the end of the effect of the surgery on him. He moved around more, no longer gave the impression of being in pain, and seemed perfectly normal. Tom had to remind himself that perfectly normal for Precious had meant vicious.

He still growled at strangers who appeared at the house or at the shop, when he was permitted to go back there, but he didn't bite anyone. And without quite realizing they were

131

doing it, they fell into the habit, "just to be sure," of clapping a muzzle on him when strangers were expected at the house or the shop.

Then something happened that cheered everybody.

Bonaparte, the Doberman pinscher with the Napoleon complex, seemed to be getting worse. Whereas before he had been content just to throw himself at the fence around the Hayneses' property when another male dog appeared, now, if he wasn't chained in the yard, he managed somehow to leap over the fence or sneak out the front door of the house when he sensed the presence of a male dog in the neighborhood. He tore the skin off his body leaping the fence, but that didn't seem to bother him.

Without thinking, Dr. Lockwood said something that enraged Mrs. Lockwood: "Well, at least it's nice to know we don't own the only crazy dog in town."

He got a five-minute lecture from Mrs. Lockwood, in which she reminded him that Precious's "problem" had been "cured." That Precious hadn't even looked as if he were going to nip anybody, much less bite, since he had had his operation. He was now, in fact, sort of a pussycat—a nice, gentle, affectionate dog who didn't run away from home and was obedient and lovable.

About ninety-five percent of that, Tom decided, was true. But it was also true that when Precious was upset—that is, if he was asleep when the doorbell rang and it shocked him—the growl that came from his massive chest was as frightening as it ever had been. And it was also true that no one went near him when he was eating. And it was entirely possible, Tom concluded, that the reason Precious hadn't even looked as if he wanted to bite somebody was because he was smart enough to know that with his muzzle, he simply couldn't.

Early one Sunday morning, when Tom was in his bedroom watching a 1930s Charlie Chan movie on television, the telephone rang. A moment later, his mother burst through his door.

"Where's Precious?" she asked. "That was Mrs. Haynes. Bonaparte's on the loose!"

"He's with Dad," Tom replied. "Dad's working on the *GIGO*."

And then he jumped out of bed. The boat was outside the fence. That meant Precious was loose. Precious wasn't a roamer, and he would stay with whomever he was with. But it would be a different matter if a strange dog, one looking for a fight, came onto what Precious considered his property. And he wasn't wearing his muzzle.

Tom pulled on a pair of jeans, jammed his feet into sneakers, and ran downstairs and through the kitchen. He jerked the door open and waved at his father.

"Put Precious inside the fence," he shouted. "Bonaparte's loose."

"Damn," his father said, and then he said it again when he saw that it was too late to get Precious inside the fence.

Bonaparte, who seemed to be walking on his toes like a ballet dancer, was coming down the fence line toward the canal. And Precious had seen him. Precious was walking up the canal toward the corner of the fence. He wasn't running, but his gait was stiff, and even from the kitchen door, Tom could hear the growling deep in Precious's chest.

It was bloodcurdling, he thought. It really was bloodcurdling. There was not half an ounce of lovable family pooch in that sound. It was the sound of a wild animal.

"Precious!" he shouted. "Precious, come!"

Precious gave no sign that he had heard him.

"That won't do any good," Dr. Lockwood called. "Get the water hose. Dogs hate to be sprayed with water."

"You be careful!" Mrs. Lockwood called out. "You don't want to get bitten."

Eighty percent of the time, the water hose was lying

sprawled across the backyard, hooked up to the faucet. Today, because they needed it in a hurry, it was inevitable that Dr. Lockwood, in one of his rare let's-clean-this-mess-up moods, had carefully coiled it on its carriage and rolled it into the garage.

It took Tom, working frantically, about a minute to get the hose carriage into the backyard, the hose screwed onto the faucet, and to run, dragging the hose behind him, across the yard to where Bonaparte and Precious were on a collision course.

Both dogs were now moving very slowly, looking like actors in a slow-motion film. Tom screamed at Precious, but Precious acted as if Tom were on the moon. The closer Precious and Bonaparte got to each other, the slower they moved.

Precious's growling was now as deep as Tom had ever heard it. He remembered everything that Dr. Harte had said about Old English sheepdogs being bred to protect their sheep. That instinct was now very evident. There was no question in Tom's mind that it was Precious's intention to kill the intruder or to die trying.

Tom was now at the fence. He had turned on the water faucet fully, but it was a long time before water had come through the empty hose to the nozzle. It was running now, but the stream was weak. It wouldn't bother a dog, much less deter him from fighting.

Tom knew what it was. The washing machine was on. When the washing machine was using water, the supply to the outside faucets was severely reduced.

"Mom," he screamed, turning around, "turn off the washing machine!"

She looked at him as if he were crazy, until she realized what he was talking about, and then she ran to the utility room. The dogs were now no more than two feet from each other, and Precious's growling was really frightening

Tom was reluctant to turn back and see what was happening. He decided that if all else failed, he'd climb the fence and swing the hose like a whip on the dogs, at least until the pressure came on, to separate them.

But when he turned around, instead of two large, ferocious dogs trying to kill each other, he saw an astonishing sight: Bonaparte, who had earned the reputation of being the neighborhood bully because of his belligerence, was lying on his back with his feet in the air and his normally perky ears flat against his skull. Instead of growling threateningly, he was whining.

Precious stood over him, as stiff as a board, but made no move to bite him. He was growling, but not as ferociously as a moment before.

Bonaparte, Tom realized, had surrendered without a fight.

The hose jumped in Tom's hand as the pressure came back on. The stream caught Precious in the shoulder, and he looked quickly at Tom. Tom directed the stream at Bonaparte. Bonaparte rolled back onto his stomach and started to crawl away.

To give Precious something besides Bonaparte to think about, Tom sprayed him with the hose. Precious, his dignity outraged, ran back toward Dr. Lockwood and the *GIGO*. Tom stopped spraying him. Precious turned around and watched Bonaparte. After crawling fifteen feet on his stomach, Bonaparte got up and ran toward his home.

"Well, I'll be damned," Dr. Lockwood said. He dropped to his knees and wrapped his arms around Precious.

"Precious, I'm proud of you," he said. "I never thought I'd see that."

Precious wagged his tail and nuzzled Dr. Lockwood in the neck.

135

CHAPTER 14

THE FIRST REAL SIGN TOM SAW THAT PRE-
cious wasn't entirely cured—that Precious, in
fact, was still both crazy and dangerous—came
four months later, when Paul, Jr., brought a girl
home from M.I.T. at the end of his sophomore year.

As Paul, Jr., explained it on the telephone, he had nothing going with the girl but a practical business arrangement
to save money and at the same time have someone to share
the long drive with. The girl was going to rent a trailer to tow
behind the Triumph. It would be loaded with furniture she
wanted to bring home from college. If she shipped it by truck
it would cost a fortune. She was willing to pay for all their gas
and food and other expenses on the road, and she would help
drive. They would drive straight through, one driving while
the other slept. They would then spend a couple of days
catching up on their sleep at the Lockwoods', maybe go fishing, and then proceed to her house, another four hundred
miles away.

It looked like a one-way deal to Tom. Getting a trailer-
load of stuff hauled halfway across the country for the price
of the gas and all the hamburgers Paul, Jr., could eat was
obviously a free ride.

The reason Tom knew so much about the cost of operating an automobile was that he had had a run-in with his
father about taking the Mustang for a Sunday excursion to a
beach ninety miles away.

"What's wrong with the beach here?" his father had
asked. "It's got water and sand and girls in bikinis."

136

"It won't cost me a dime," Tom had replied. "Fred and Charley are going to pay for the gas."

"You come up with a good reason why the company should make Fred and Charley a gift of, oh, say fifty dollars, and you can take the company's car," his father had said.

"What do you mean, a gift of fifty dollars?"

Dr. Lockwood had then seated him before the shop computer and given him the data he was to feed it: how much the Mustang had cost; how much they could expect to get for it when they sold it after three years; the cost of license plates and insurance over three years; the cost of scheduled maintenance, including oil and filter changes; how many miles the Mustang went on one gallon of gasoline; how much a gallon of gasoline cost; and, as a factor, all of this related to driving the car 12,000 miles a year for three years.

"Okay," his father had said. "Now ask it how much it costs to operate that Mustang by the mile."

Tom had typed: QUERY: COST PER MILE?

The computer screen had gone blank for a couple of seconds, and then the answer had appeared on the screen: COST PER MILE: $00.34844.

"That much?" Tom had asked, really surprised.

"The computer never lies," his father had replied, very pleased with himself. "And you want to go one hundred eighty miles round trip, right?"

"Right."

"See how much that costs," his father had said.

The computer had promptly informed them that one hundred eighty miles at $00.34844 per mile came to $62.71920.

"Now, since one hundred eighty miles is almost exactly ten gallons worth of gas, subtract fifteen dollars. Ten gallons at a buck and a half."

The answer was $47.71920.

"Call it forty-seven seventy-two," Dr. Lockwood had said. "I was off a couple of bucks."

"You made your point," Tom had said.

"Didn't I?" Dr. Lockwood had said smugly. "The cheapest thing you put in a car is gas."

Tom looked forward eagerly to explaining to Paul, Jr., how much it had cost him to have someone share the driving.

When he saw the girl, however, he decided she was worth whatever it had cost. She was a perky little brunette with a wicked sense of humor, obviously too good for Paul, Jr. She made an instant hit with Mrs. Lockwood by insisting that she would do the dishes, and with Dr. Lockwood by passing on the regards of one of his professors.

"How'd you come to meet him?"

"I'm in his class," Deborah Young said.

"You're a math major?" Dr. Lockwood asked, delighted.

"Yes, sir," she said.

There were few people Dr. Lockwood liked better than good-looking, polite young women who called him sir and who were smart enough to be accepted into the classes of an M.I.T. professor he admired.

Also, Deborah Young was familiar with the shop computer.

"We've got one at school," she said. "But there's never been any free time available on it for me to play with it."

"In the morning, if you like," Dr. Lockwood replied, "Tom can take you over to the shop and show you how it works. He's getting pretty good with it."

"Oh," Deborah Young said, "would you, Tom?"

"Sure," Tom said. Deborah, he decided, had just joined that long line of delightful females whom a cruel fate had seen born several years too early for him.

But Precious hated Deborah Young.

"Just to be safe," when they saw Paul, Jr.'s car rolling up the driveway, they had lured Precious into the library, put the muzzle on him, and locked him inside. He would be let

138

announced that dogs were splendid
and offered the hope that Paul, Jr.,
about "that young woman." And when
cious had bared his teeth and growled
e had tried to put the muzzle on him,
d said that she would growl herself if
muzzle on her, and the proof that all
s announcing his displeasure was
d let Tom put "that nasty thing" on

arguing with her, so Tom simply

rned from dragging Deborah's
s seemed as excitedly happy to
, and when, to see what would
ut on Precious's muzzle, Pre-
im do it.
ome home, however, Precious
Paul, Jr., and worried Tom.
with him in the Triumph to
e plant. Because he didn't
ut the roof on the car and
way up. That way Precious
l, Jr., was inside the bus

ind the wheel, he noticed
Too hot in here for you,
crank down the window
that the vinyl upholstery
several places.
ock and dismay when
w himself at the win-
past the car on the
ght. That didn't seem
bite her, he bit the

out after supper, when the excitement of Paul, Jr.'s return,
and with a stranger, had had a chance to die down.

Paul, Jr., let Precious out of the library after Dr.
Lockwood had warned him not to take off his muzzle. Precious sniffed Paul, Jr., and wagged his tail briefly. Then he
trotted quickly into the living room to investigate the source
of the strange voice and smell.

"He's enormous!" Deborah Young said.

"Be a little careful with him, Deborah," Mrs. Lockwood
said. "Sometimes Precious is a little strange with strangers."

He was strange with Deborah. He went straight to her
and stood six inches from her and just looked at her. His
hindquarters were not wagging.

"It'll take him some time to get used to you," Mrs.
Lockwood said.

"I understand," Deborah said.

When Precious didn't move for more than a minute,
and just stood in front of Deborah's chair, Mrs. Lockwood
told Tom to make him sit down.

Precious still didn't move when Tom told him to come,
and when Tom went to him to haul him away by the collar,
he felt that Precious's body was tense.

"Bad boy!" Tom said.

There was a faint but unmistakable growl in Precious's
throat.

"I can't understand that," Deborah said. "Most dogs
like me."

"He's just not used to visitors," Mrs. Lockwood said.

"Maybe if I gave him something to eat?" Deborah asked.

"If we took his muzzle off so that he could eat," Tom
said, "he'd probably eat your hand."

"Tom!" Mrs. Lockwood said.

Deborah Young looked at Tom. He saw understanding
in her eyes.

"I'm really sorry for you," she said.

When Dr. Lockwood had a moment alone with Tom, he asked him, "Was he growling? Or was that my imagination?"

"Growling and as stiff as a board," Tom said.

"Well, she's a stranger, and he's jealous," Dr. Lockwood said.

"We're going to have to keep the muzzle on him," Tom said.

"Yeah," his father said. "At least that."

Deborah slept in Paul, Jr.'s bed, and Paul, Jr., slept with Tom. Tom had inherited a double bed from his parents, but he had grown used to sleeping sprawled across it, and in his sleep, he kept bumping into his brother and waking up.

And every time he woke up, he was aware that Precious, who normally would have tried to get into bed with them, was lying on the floor with his nose to the crack under the door. Whenever Precious heard a spring creak, or Deborah made some other sound in Paul, Jr.'s room, Precious growled. They'd taken his muzzle off as soon as they'd closed the door to their room and his growl was now loud and un pleasant.

"Maybe it's some perfume she's wearing, or so thing," Paul, Jr., said. Tom hadn't known he was awa

"No," Tom said. "I wish it were that, but it's no

"I thought he was fixed," Paul, Jr., said.

"Until you came home," Tom said, "I though'

"Well, don't blame me!"

"I'm not blaming you," Tom said. "It's nol

In the morning, when Paul, Jr., tried to muzzle on, he growled and bared his teeth.

"Damn dog!" Paul, Jr., said. "You're muzzle him, Tom. He just turned on me."

Precious growled when Tom appro muzzle, but there was something about know he wasn't going to take a bite at hin. was just to tell Tom he didn't like being muzzle.

Deborah stayed one more night. As long as sh

140

Jr.'s girl friend, judges of character wasn't getting serious

Tom told her that Pre at Paul, Jr., because h Grandmother Lockwoo somebody tried to put a Precious was doing wa that he had sat there an him.

There was no point i shut up.

When Paul, Jr., ret trailer to her home, Precio see him as he ever had bee happen, Paul, Jr., tried to cious just sat there and let h

Two days after he had c did something that infuriated

Paul, Jr., took Precious pick up packages sent from want to muzzle Precious, he rolled the windows nearly all th would get enough air while Pau terminal.

When he came out and got be first that Precious was panting. boy?" he asked, and leaned over to on the passenger side. Then he saw trim on the door had been ripped i

He was still staring at it in s Precious, snarling and growling, thr dow. Paul, Jr., saw a woman walkin sidewalk jump aside in surprise and fr to satisfy Precious. Since he couldn't upholstery trim on the door.

142

there brar did He

Then Paul, Jr., drove to the shop and told his father and Tom what had happened. "There are two things you can do," Tom said. "You can put a muzzle on him when you take him in the car, which is a pretty good idea, anyway."

"Or what?"

"You can take him to Dr. Harte and have him put down," Tom said.

"What do you mean, put down?"

"You know what I mean," Tom replied. "Dad and I did it the last time. Now it's your turn. Once is enough for me."

"Well, if you think I'm going to have him killed just because he tried to protect my car—"

"Then put a muzzle on him, and keep it on him whenever there's the slightest chance he'll take a bite out of somebody," Tom said.

Precious, who knew both that he was in trouble with Paul, Jr., and that he was the subject of the conversation, walked over to Paul, Jr., and nudged him. Paul, Jr., looked down at him.

"What do you want?" he asked.

Precious handed him his paw.

Paul, Jr., squatted down and took it. "I may never forgive you for eating my upholstery," he said. "But don't you worry, boy. I'm not going to have you killed for it."

"That was a cheap shot, Paul," Tom snapped.

"You make me sick, the way you talk so easily about killing him," Paul, Jr., flared. "The only thing wrong with him is that he's got an overdeveloped sense of being a shepherd. He's just trying to do his job, that's all."

Dr. Lockwood just stood there, listening to his sons.

Tom was faced with the choice between taking a punch at his brother or leaving the room. He left the room and went into the office and sat down at the computer. He didn't have any work for the computer, but he had learned enough about it to be able to play with it. He had reprogrammed the response function, for example. Whenever insufficient or irrelevant data was inserted, it had been programmed to flash INSUFFICIENT DATA or IRRELEVANT DATA on the screen. Tom had reprogrammed it, so that GIGO, DUMMY, GIGO! now came onto the screen.

It was now his intention to change another response. The machine, when first turned on, flashed GOOD MORNING. YOUR MODEL 909D COMPUTER IS EAGER TO GO TO WORK!

That reminded Tom of a television commercial, and he hated it. Tomorrow, when his father or Mr. Lopez turned it on, they were going to be greeted with: IT'S ABOUT TIME YOU SHOWED UP!

He was halfway through the necessary steps when he became aware that his father was standing behind him, looking over his shoulder.

"Wise guy," his father said, when he saw what Tom had done.

"Want me to change it back?"

"No, it'll make Lopez laugh," his father said.

"You got something for me to do?" Tom asked.

"I've got something to say to you," Dr. Lockwood said.

"What?" Tom asked. He could see that his father was very serious.

"Paul was dead wrong just now," Dr. Lockwood said.

"I know he was," Tom replied. "No problem."

"Yeah, there is," Dr. Lockwood said.

"I don't understand."

"There are only two people who have had the intellectual honesty to see Precious for what he is. You and I. The others are unable or unwilling to see him for what he really is."

"I suppose you're right," Tom said.

"And neither you nor I have the guts, or whatever it takes, to take that giant step from intellectual conclusion to physical action."

"What do you mean by that?"

144

"Neither you nor I can find it in ourselves to take Precious back to Dr. Harte and have him put down," Dr. Lockwood said. "I think that makes us worse than Paul, Jr., or Grandmother Lockwood."

"We'll just have to do it, that's all," Tom said.

"Yes, we will," Dr. Lockwood said. "Anytime you're ready, let me know, and we'll go down there together. Or if I find the courage first, I'll let you know."

"If only he'd stay vicious," Tom said.

"I'm sure Dr. Jekyll was charming and lovable when his fangs were retracted," Dr. Lockwood said.

"Let's make a deal," Tom said. "Let's be fair. He really hasn't bitten anybody. Let's give him that much. Let's keep the muzzle on him, keep him away from strangers. Try to do what we can. If it doesn't work, the very next time he hurts somebody, that's it."

"Okay. I agree," Dr. Lockwood said. "But I can't help thinking it's one of those promises we both mean right now, but which we'll feel a lot different about when it's time to really go through with it."

CHAPTER 15

PRECIOUS GOT THROUGH THE REST OF THE summer without biting anyone. Everyone took great pains to make sure that he was muzzled anytime he left the property or the shop, or whenever there were strangers around. No one went near him when he was eating.

He developed a new nasty habit. He had always liked to go into the downstairs bathroom so he could lay his belly against the cool tile floor. And he had always made it perfectly clear that he objected to being chased out of the bathroom when someone had to use it. Now he started to growl at anyone who ordered him out of the bathroom.

That was bad enough, but it got worse. Sometimes, whether by accident or on purpose, he managed to close the bathroom door when he was inside. Once Tom, not thinking about Precious, pushed open the door to the bathroom. Precious was asleep inside. The door hit him. He jumped, snarling, to his feet and attacked the door. Tom realized, as he hastily pulled it shut again, that Precious would have bitten whoever had pushed the door against him if he could have.

That was the first time the skin on Tom's neck had really "crawled in fear." He'd read that expression twenty times in books and magazines but had never before thought it was anything but a writer's active imagination. The animal behind the door was wild and meant him harm, and his skin *had* crawled. It was not the same dog who crept carefully into his bed and lay his head on the pillow and affectionately licked his ear.

146

Tom realized that the whole sickening affair was coming to a head, but, like his father, he just couldn't find the heart to load a trusting Precious into the Mustang and take him to Dr. Harte.

Tom thought about it a good deal when his father went off for three weeks on what he called "one of his globe girdlers." Every eighteen months or so, it was necessary for Dr. Lockwood to "get out into the field." It was important to the company, for Wallwood Microtronics offices liked to show off the chief research engineer to their customers, and it was important to his father, because he could see firsthand the problems the "people in the field" had working with the equipment he had designed.

He flew around the world, flying first to New York and then to Europe, from Europe to the Near East, and then on to Australia and Japan, Korea, and Hawaii. Finally, he flew home by way of San Francisco.

While his father was gone, Tom was worried about his mother having an incident with Precious when he was out of the house. The Lopezes took their vacation while Dr. Lockwood was away, so Precious couldn't spend his days asleep in the shop.

To Tom's enormous relief, nothing happened while Dr. Lockwood was gone. The only thing out of the ordinary was that Precious spent most of his time behind Dr. Lockwood's chair in the living room. He left that dark and protected corner only to eat, or to briefly visit the backyard. Tom decided it was because he missed his cave under the computer keyboard in the shop, but for some reason, it bothered him. It was another strange change in behavior.

Tom was very relieved when Dr. Lockwood called from New York and said he would arrive at the airport at half-past nine that night.

When Tom met him at the airport, he saw how tired his father was, despite his best efforts to be cheerful and full of life. "Someone should have locked up the Wright brothers,"

Dr. Lockwood said as Tom drove him home. "If God wanted man to fly he would have given him wings."

"How would you have gone around the world, then?" Tom asked, chuckling.

"I would have gone around on a ship," Dr. Lockwood said. "Sleeping in a bed, not sitting up in a chair. I would have been plied with elegant food, served at a table with linen, crystal, and silver, instead of having a plastic tray loaded with plastic food spilled on my lap. Bring back the ocean liners!"

"You're all worn out, huh?"

"Yeah," Dr. Lockwood said. "I really am. It would appear that your old man ain't as young as he once was, Tom. I really am beat."

Tom nodded.

"Don't say anything to your mother, Tom," he added, after a moment. "I'll be all right in a couple of days. What's probably bothering me is jet lag." And then he made a joke of that: "Jet lag is God's way of telling man that he wasn't meant to fly."

Precious, when he saw Dr. Lockwood, acted like a puppy. Tom couldn't remember having seen him act so happy in a long time, and he decided that was the reason Precious had stayed behind his father's chair. In other words, Precious had simply missed Dr. Lockwood and had gone to the place where he expected to find him. That night, Precious elected to sleep in the corridor outside Tom's parents' bedroom rather than with Tom. There was something really touching about it. Precious the sheepdog was delighted that one of his wandering sheep had returned to the herd and wanted to make sure he didn't stray again.

At breakfast the next morning, Dr. Lockwood said that he was going to take a day or two off, before going back to work. And he meant *off*. He was not going fishing. He was not going to fix anything that was broken or look at anything that needed looking at. He was going to lie on the couch in

148

the living room, drink hard liquor, and watch soap operas on television. If there were any calls for him, the callers were to be told that he had last been seen riding off into the sunset, aboard an elephant in Bombay, India.

He was on the couch before Tom went off to school, and he was asleep on the couch when Tom came home. Precious lay beside the couch. *He* didn't seem to have moved, either.

"Dad must be really tired," Tom said to his mother.

"He's been drinking all afternoon," Mrs. Lockwood replied. "That's why he's asleep." But she was obviously more concerned than critical. She told Tom that she was making a standing rib of beef for their dinner. "That's his favorite meal," she said. "It should cheer him up."

Tom heard the television go on when it was time for the evening news, and he walked into the living room.

"Ah, the bartender," his father said.

"How do you feel?"

"There's nothing wrong with me that a stiff scotch and water won't fix," Dr. Lockwood said. "I must have one of those exotic Asian viruses we keep hearing about."

Tom made his father a drink. When he carried it to him, Dr. Lockwood told Tom to let him know when the roast was done, so that he could make the Yorkshire pudding.

"Your mother is a splendid cook," he said. "Her Yorkshire pudding is the exception that proves the rule."

Tom had been stationed by the oven to watch the meat thermometer. When it registered "rare," he took the roast from the oven and called to his father. "Are you going to make the Yorkshire pudding, Dad?"

"Be right there," his father said, and a moment later, with Precious at his heels, he came into the kitchen.

Tom had taken the roast beef out of the roasting pan, so that his father could get at the drippings.

"That smells great!" Dr. Lockwood said, taking a wooden spoon from a drawer.

Then he turned and faced Tom. "I must have had a lot

149

more scotch than I thought," he said. "I'm plastered. I'm going to have to sit down before I fall down."

"Go ahead," Tom said. "I know how to make the pudding."

"Yeah, sure you do," his father said, and walked out of the kitchen.

Tom picked up the wooden spoon and started to scrape the roasting pan. A moment later, he heard a strange thud in the dining room. He decided his father must have bumped into the dining-room table.

"You all right, Dad?" Tom called. When he got no reply, he called "Dad?" again, and then he pushed open the swinging door to the dining room.

Dr. Lockwood was lying on the dining-room floor on his stomach, his legs askew, his right arm stretched out over his head. Precious was sniffing his face, trying to figure out what was going on.

For a moment, Tom thought that his father had passed out drunk. But as quickly as that thought had come into his mind, he put it out. He had never seen his father really drunk, and he hadn't seemed drunk in the kitchen, just tired.

Tom dropped to his knees beside his father.

Precious growled at him.

"It's all right, Precious," Tom said automatically, even though he knew that it was not all right, that something was seriously wrong with his father. His father was pale, and there was a strange sweat on his forehead.

More frightened than he had ever been, he put his hand under his father's chest and rolled him over on his back, then put his ear to his chest. He could hear the heart beating.

Tom got up and ran to the stairs.

"Mom, call the cops and get an ambulance!" he screamed. "Dad passed out in the dining room."

Instead of calling the police, she came running down

the stairs and into the dining room. Precious stood over Dr. Lockwood and snarled at her.

"Oh, my God!" she said.

"Call the cops and get an ambulance!" Tom said. He was afraid that she was going to ignore Precious and try to get to Dr. Lockwood. But she turned and ran from the room, and Tom could hear her dialing the telephone in the kitchen.

Dr. Lockwood groaned and seemed to be trying to speak.

Tom went to him. Precious alternately whined and snarled. Tom realized he was going to have to get the muzzle on the dog before the ambulance came. He lowered his ear to his father's mouth.

"I didn't have *that* much to drink," his father said, his voice faint and puzzled. "I don't seem to be able to move. Will you help me get up?"

"An ambulance is on the way," Tom said.

"I don't need an ambulance," Dr. Lockwood said, barely audible. "I'm just a little tired, that's all."

Tom said, "Just to be sure, Dad."

Whatever was wrong with his father, it wasn't simply fatigue. His father closed his eyes. Tom was terrified.

He wondered what was keeping his mother. She came into the dining room a minute later, just as Tom heard, far off, the wail of a siren.

"I called Dr. Sheldon," Mrs. Lockwood said. "He's going to meet us at the emergency room. He said to make sure your father doesn't swallow his tongue and to throw a blanket over him."

"Stay away from him," Tom said. "Precious is all upset, and we don't need you bitten right now."

He took the blanket from his mother and started to spread it over his father. In his haste, he moved too quickly to suit Precious, and Precious nipped at his hand. At the last moment, as Precious's teeth closed on the fleshy heel of his hand, Precious seemed to understand either that Tom meant no harm or that he wasn't supposed to bite him, for he dropped Tom's hand as quickly as he had bitten it—but not before his sharp canine tooth had opened a gash in Tom's hand as deep as the gash it had made in Colonel Walker's ear.

Tom quickly put his hand behind his back, so his mother wouldn't see it. Then he told her to keep the ambulance crew out until he got the muzzle on Precious.

She went to the door, and he went to the kitchen and got the muzzle. He was afraid that Precious would give him trouble about putting on the muzzle, but Precious was in one of his I-know-I've-done-wrong-and-I'll-be-good-from-now-on moods, and he accepted the muzzle without argument.

Once it was on him, Tom ran to the library door and called to him. Reluctantly, Precious came and allowed himself to be shut in behind the door. And just in time, for the siren sound was now right outside the house, and the doorbell went off, and Precious began to throw himself at the door and whine and snarl under the muzzle.

What Tom had thought was an unusually noisy siren turned out to be two sirens. A police car had answered the emergency call, too.

Tom stood by, terrified, as he watched the ambulance crew working on his father. His mother leaned against the wall, holding her hand over her mouth. The medical technicians connected various kinds of sensors to Dr. Lockwood's body and relayed the readings by radio to the emergency room at the hospital. They covered Dr. Lockwood's face with an oxygen mask, loaded him onto a stretcher, covered him with a blanket, picked up the stretcher, and trotted out of the house to the ambulance.

"I'm going to go with your father," Mrs. Lockwood announced. "You call Paul, Jr., and Barbara and tell them what's happened, and then come to the hospital."

It wasn't until Tom tried to telephone that he

realized how badly Precious had bitten him. When he took the bitten hand from his pocket, he brought the blood-sticky pocket with it. He looked down at his trousers; they were badly bloodstained.

He went to the kitchen, washed the hand as well as he could, and put a butterfly bandage on it. Then he changed his pants. He didn't call Paul, Jr., or Barbara, despite his mother's order. It would be better to wait until they knew something. Calling them now would only upset them. There was nothing either one of them could do to help.

Tom got into the Mustang and drove to the hospital. He parked the car and went into the emergency entrance, through two heavy glass doors. He had forgotten about his bitten hand and used it to push open the door. Not only did it hurt, but it started bleeding again.

He wrapped a handkerchief over it and looked for somebody who could tell him where to find his parents. He encountered the emergency room chief nurse, a formidable woman in her fifties.

"Your father's in intensive care," she said. "And you'd be in the way. What did you do to your hand?"

Even as he protested it was just a little scratch, she took it in her strong hands, discarded the handerchief, and tore off the butterfly bandage. "I don't want you either scaring your mother or dripping blood all over our polished linoleum," she said, dragging him into a treatment room, where she cleaned and properly bandaged the wound.

"How'd you get bitten?" she asked.

"Our dog was protecting my father," Tom said. "He didn't know what was going on."

"Well, you can't blame him for that, I suppose," the nurse said. Then she told him to go to the waiting room. "I'm sure Dr. Sheldon will be out as soon as he can," she said.

The waiting room was on the other side of the intensive care ward from the emergency room. The walls of the intensive care ward had several large windows, and as he passed

153

he could see into one of the interior cubicles, where his father, connected to an awesome display of wires and tubing, lay in a bed. There was no one with him.

And then a hand touched his shoulder, and Tom turned and looked at Dr. Sheldon.

"How is he?" Tom asked, his voice right on the edge of breaking.

"Come on, and see for yourself," Dr. Sheldon said. "I want you to hear what I have to say to him, anyway."

He led Tom into the intensive care cubicle.

"How do you feel?" Dr. Sheldon asked Dr. Lockwood.

"Lousy," Dr. Lockwood said faintly. There was a plastic device in his nostrils, which made his voice sound very nasal.

"That's not surprising," Dr. Sheldon said, "seeing how close you came to taking a ride to the boneyard."

"I admire your bedside manner," Dr. Lockwood said.

"I don't feel sorry for you," Dr. Sheldon said. "I feel sorry for Tom, and for your wife, but not for you. I told you this was liable to happen."

"What did the electrocardiogram show?" Dr. Lockwood asked, and Tom saw that he wanted to change the subject.

"The cardiologist and I agree that there's nothing wrong with your heart. The problem is in your head."

"What happened to him?" Tom asked.

"He's got what they call phlebitis," Dr. Sheldon said. "Very roughly, it's a circulatory condition in which blood settles in the leg. We don't really know much about it, but we do know how to treat it. All you have to do is take a blood thinner—"

"Rat poison," Dr. Lockwood said.

"Yes, it's rat poison, same chemical," Dr. Sheldon said. "And the rat poison keeps the blood thin, so blood clots won't form. The second thing you do for people who have phlebitis is convince them not to sit in one place for longer than, say, forty-five minutes at a time, unless their legs are elevated.

Your old man, Tom, shouldn't have to be told that liquids run downhill."

"I'm not sure I like your talking this way in front of my son," Dr. Lockwood said, very testily.

"Either I tell him," Dr. Sheldon said, "or I tell Madame Lockwood. One or the other."

"Okay," Dr. Lockwood said. "I seem to be at your mercy."

"So what does this genius of a father of yours do, Tom? Let me tell you. He stops taking the rat poison because it makes him bleed a lot when he cuts himself shaving—"

"It also makes a little bruise look like someone ran over you with a truck," Dr. Lockwood said.

"Right. It does that, too," said Dr. Sheldon. "So he stops taking the medicine I prescribed. And then he gets on an airplane, and sits in what is almost precisely the wrong position for someone suffering from phlebitis, and flies around the world. He probably stopped in major cities along the way to sit for hours in front of a computer keyboard, which is also exactly the wrong position for a phlebitic. Right?"

"Okay, I've learned my lesson," Dr. Lockwood said.

"I hope so. Two out of three people who pass a blood clot the way you did don't make it to the hospital. Will you take my word for that, Paul, or will I have to show you the data?"

"Is he going to be all right?" Tom asked.

"He's going to be weak for a while, and I'm going to really thin his blood down, but, presuming we don't have a repetition of his remarkably stupid behavior, we can keep him around for a while," Dr. Sheldon said. "I have one other little bit of cheerful advice for you. Don't let yourself get excited. The one thing you don't need is a heart attack."

"You really had to say all this in front of Tom?"

"Absolutely, because if you don't fly straight, don't take your rat poison, don't walk a couple of miles a day, and continue sitting for hours in front of a computer, Tom is going to squeal on you to me, and then I will *promptly* run to

Madame Lockwood, *and* Paul, Jr., *and* Barbara. You get the picture?"

"And I'll squeal, Dad," Tom said. "You can bet on that."

"I have nurtured a viper," Dr. Lockwood said.

"What about liquor?" Tom asked. "He had a lot to drink before he fell down."

"That probably kept him alive," Dr. Sheldon said. "Alcohol thins the blood. He can have all he wants to drink."

"You will tell my wife that, won't you?" Dr. Lockwood said. "She wouldn't believe it from me."

"Yeah, I'll tell her, when I tell her that what's wrong with you is exhaustion, and that what you need is three weeks off doing nothing. I will also lie and tell her the rat poison is to lower your blood pressure. But that's as far as I'm going, bosom buddy or no bosom buddy. I don't want to carry your casket, Paul, and I just hope you realize how close to that we've come."

"He'll behave," Tom said.

"Now we'll go tell lies to your wife," Dr. Sheldon said. He took Tom's arm and led him out of the glass-walled cubicle.

CHAPTER 16

PAUL'S GOING TO BE ALL RIGHT, CARO-
line," Dr. Sheldon said when he went up to Mrs.
Lockwood in the waiting room. "You were very
nearly a widow, to be brutal about it, but we have
his condition under control. He's out of danger, and if he
behaves himself, there's no reason why he can't live to be a
hundred." Mrs. Lockwood started to cry, and then asked if
she could see her husband.

"You can see him in the morning," Dr. Sheldon said.
"What you're going to do now is go home, take two of the pills
I'm going to give Tom for you, and go to bed. In the morning,
I'll want to talk to you about how we'll take care of Paul from
now on."

"What was it, a heart attack?" she asked, sniffling.

"No. His heart's in fine shape. I'm not going to talk in
detail about it now, but what really happened to him is a
form of exhaustion. The cure for exhaustion is rest."

"I've never been so frightened in my life," she said.

"He hates to admit it, but I don't think Paul has,
either," Dr. Sheldon said. "Now go home, go to bed, and I'll
see you here in the morning."

Mrs. Lockwood impulsively kissed Dr. Sheldon and
thanked him, and then allowed Tom to take her out to the
Mustang. Tom went back into the hospital and got a small
box with two pills from Dr. Sheldon.

"She's in emotional shock," Dr. Sheldon said to him.
"What shape are you in?"

"I'm all right," Tom said.

"What about the dog?" Dr. Sheldon asked.

"What about him?"

"I heard, from Mrs. Crump, about your hand."

"The dog was in emotional shock, too, I guess," Tom said. "I don't think he intended to do as much damage as he did."

"You're going to have to make a decision about him," Dr. Sheldon said. "You heard what I said about keeping your Dad from getting excited?"

"Yes, sir."

"I can't tell you what to do, Tom, but I must tell you that your parents aren't really capable right now of making unpleasant decisions."

"Okay," Tom said, "I understand."

"Give her both those pills at once. In fifteen minutes, she'll get very sleepy, and she'll sleep like a stone for twelve hours. Don't wake her in the morning. Whenever she wakes up and can come over here will be all right."

"Yes, sir."

The proof that his mother was in emotional shock was that she didn't ask Tom about Barbara or Paul, Jr. She seemed to be in a daze when they got home. She took Dr. Sheldon's pills without comment. She walked around the house, straightening things up for ten minutes, and then, as Dr. Sheldon had predicted, she got very sleepy and announced that she was going to bed.

Tom waited for five minutes, until he felt sure she was actually in bed and asleep, and then he went into the library. Precious greeted him at the door. He was still in one of his I-know-I've-done-wrong moods. Tom took the muzzle off him, sat down at the desk, and got out the telephone book.

He called Barbara first, and then Paul, Jr., and then Charley Walton, and told them what had happened. While Tom talked on the telephone, Precious put his head on Tom's lap, and then, when he got tired, lay down on the carpet with his head resting on Tom's foot.

Barbara got a little hysterical and set out for home as soon as they hung up. She arrived at half-past two in the morning. Precious, asleep in Tom's room, heard her coming through the front door and rushed snarling to protect the house from the unknown intruder. Once he recognized Barbara, however, he acted like a friendly puppy.

Tom was afraid that his mother would be awakened by the noise, but whatever Dr. Sheldon had given her kept her asleep. Barbara, naturally, wanted details that Tom had not given her over the telephone. That put Tom in the uncomfortable position of deciding whether it would be best to tell her the truth, the whole truth, and nothing but the truth, or to give her the laundered version of the story that Dr. Sheldon had given their mother.

He decided that telling Barbara the whole truth would be the same thing as telling his mother the whole truth, for Barbara would certainly spill the beans to their mother. He gave her the laundered version, and he repeated that version at ten the next morning, when he picked up Paul, Jr., at the airport.

Tom drove Paul, Jr., directly to the hospital from the airport. Barbara had taken their mother there in the station wagon.

Dr. Lockwood was still in the cubicle in the intensive care ward and still connected to the science-fiction-movie array of monitoring devices by a web of cables and tubes. He had a hypodermic needle taped to the back of his hand, through which a saline solution and "liquid rat poison" dripped into his vein.

The oxygen apparatus that had been in his nostrils was gone, however, and Dr. Lockwood was in good spirits. He reported that he had amused himself through the night by "breaking up the nurses' poker game." He had held his breath, causing the respiratory monitor at the nurses' station to jump and bringing them on the run.

But just as soon as Dr. Lockwood had told them this

story, they were all run out of the intensive care ward. Visitors were discouraged in intensive care, and the rules had been bent as far as the nurses were willing to allow.

They all went home. When they got there, Tom's mother said, "I can't understand why Mother Lockwood hasn't been to the hospital," and Tom was forced to confess that he had forgotten to call her and let her know what had happened. He had also forgotten to call the Lopezes and Colonel Switzer. For this, he got a good tongue lashing from his mother, his brother, and his sister.

Grandmother Lockwood arrived within the hour, and she was the only one who didn't seem furious with him. She even explained why the others were so angry. "They want to be angry with somebody, or something, for what happened to your dad," she said. "You made yourself available. Personally, I think you handled things superbly."

Mr. and Mrs. Walton arrived an hour after Grandmother Lockwood, and fifteen minutes after they'd walked through the door, Colonel Switzer drove up. The house was full of people. Precious was kept muzzled and in the library.

There was nothing that anybody could do for Dr. Lockwood or, for that matter, for Mrs. Lockwood. There was a lot of frantic activity for the next forty-eight hours: the hauling of food from fast-food joints to the house to spare Mrs. Lockwood the need to cook; the scheduling of who was allowed to go to the hospital for the three-times-a-day, fifteen-minute visits to Dr. Lockwood; and the nearly constant answering of the telephone as Dr. Lockwood's friends and associates, hearing the news, called to ask about his condition and to offer to help in any way they could. There was also a steady line of florists' delivery trucks to the house. Flowers weren't permitted in the intensive care ward, so they were taken to the house.

On the morning of his third day in the hospital, Dr. Lockwood was released from intensive care and put into a regular room. He could now have all the visitors he wanted, for as long as he wanted. Tom saw that in the fifteen-minute visits everybody had said everything that could be said, and both the visitors and his father were bored with each other.

Colonel Switzer was the first to leave, and the Waltons left the same afternoon. Then Barbara and Paul, Jr., left. Barbara had her job to worry about, and, she said, "There's nothing I can really do to help. I'll come back when Dad's out of the hospital." Paul, Jr., had already missed important classes and couldn't afford to miss any more. Almost as quickly as they had arrived, all the visitors had left, and, with the exception of Dr. Lockwood's being in the hospital, things were back to normal.

Seven days after he had been carried into the hospital, Tom's father was sitting on the bed, fully dressed and ready to go home when Tom stopped by on his way to school. "Sheldon said that if he had told me last night I was about through with this place," Dr. Lockwood said, "I would have insisted on going home last night."

Tom drove his father home. Precious greeted him at the door and whined with joy at seeing him. Dr. Lockwood flatly rejected his wife's suggestion that he go to bed and installed himself on the couch in the living room.

After school, Tom went by the bus station and then went to the shop to tell the Lopezes that his father was out of the hospital. They already knew; Dr. Lockwood had been to the shop.

"Dr. Sheldon called me," Mr. Lopez said, "and said that he had made a deal with your father. He can come here one hour in the morning and one hour in the afternoon. I had to give him my word that I'd call if your father stayed sixty seconds more than he's supposed to."

"I guess Dr. Sheldon figured just being in the house would drive Dad crazy," Tom replied.

"That's what he said," Mr. Lopez said.

When Tom went home, he found his parents in the living room. Mrs. Lockwood was handing his father a drink. Precious was stretched out on the carpet beside the couch.

"I could learn to like living like this," his father said. "With medical permission to drink all I want to, and having it served by a very pretty waitress."

"He didn't say you could have all you wanted," Mrs. Lockwood corrected him. "He said you should have one drink before lunch and another before dinner, and that one or two more wouldn't hurt you."

"That's three more drinks than you usually allow me," Dr. Lockwood said. "Now go do something feminine; I want to have a word in private with our number-two son."

Dr. Lockwood waited until Mrs. Lockwood was gone. Then he took out his wallet.

"Money, they say, can never repay something that's done out of love. But I think it's way ahead of whatever else there is." He handed Tom a fifty-dollar bill.

"I won't be a hypocrite and say I don't want that," Tom said. "But you don't owe it to me."

"You came through in this mess like a champ, Tom," his father said. "And I don't mean only the errands everybody has had you running. You earned the money just running errands. Take it. I can't repay you for the other things you did."

"Okay," Tom said. "Thanks." He took the money.

"And tonight I want you to get out of here. Go do something. If you can find a girl who can put up with your company, take her to the movies or something. Take the night off, is what I'm saying. That's an order."

"I hear and obey, master," Tom said with a chuckle.

"Just so we understand each other," Dr. Lockwood said, "I am faithfully going to take my rat poison and a three-mile walk a day, and I told Mr. Lopez to buy a timer so that I won't be able to sit more than thirty minutes at a time without hearing an unpleasant bell."

162

"Just so we understand each other," Tom said, "you'd better, or I'll squeal."

The cold truth of the matter was that all the girls in the senior class who Tom would have enjoyed taking to the movies had more or less semipermanent relationships with other guys, so instead of making a date, he went to Beach Billiards & Bowling. He bowled a couple of games and then played nine-ball until nearly midnight with a bunch of guys his mother disliked. She equated the guys who shot pool at Beach Billiards & Bowling with crooked pool sharks who preyed on innocent young boys. The proof that she was wrong was that Tom walked out of Beach Billiards & Bowling with fifteen dollars more than he had walked in with.

The lights were on in the living room and in the kitchen when he drove into the driveway. He was surprised, because he thought that his parents would have gone to bed early the first night after his father had come home from the hospital.

When he walked into the kitchen, his father was standing by the sink, sipping at a glass dark with whiskey.

Tom knew that something was seriously wrong even before he saw his father's other hand, which was wrapped in a heavy blood-soaked bandage.

"What happened?" Tom asked.

His father held out the bandaged hand.

"I forgot he was asleep on the floor beside the couch," his father said, "and I kicked him when I got up to go to the john."

"Oh, God!" Tom said.

"He did a job on me," Dr. Lockwood said. "Sheldon had to put five stitches in me. And he did a job on your mother, too."

"He bit Mom?"

"No. But he pushed her over the edge," Dr. Lockwood said. "She really flipped her lid. She called the cops out here, and when they came, she demanded that they shoot him, and then she got really nasty when they told her they were sorry, but putting him down was our responsibility, not theirs."

"Where is she?"

"In bed. Sheldon gave her a couple of pills he says will make her sleep for twelve hours."

"Where's the dog?"

"In the library," Dr. Lockwood said.

"You remember our agreement," Tom said. "I'll take him to Dr. Harte first thing in the morning."

"I think you're going to have to, Tom," Dr. Lockwood said.

"I'll do it," Tom said.

"Sheldon had a hell of a time with my hand," Dr. Lockwood said. "That rat poison really makes me bleed."

"He also said you weren't to get excited," Tom said.

"He wanted to give me the same kind of pills he gave your mother," Dr. Lockwood said. "I told him I would prefer my tranquilizers and sleeping pills in liquid form." He raised the glass.

Tom didn't reply.

"And he said that if I didn't do something about Precious," Dr. Lockwood said slowly, "he would get Paul, Jr., down here and have him take care of it."

"I'll take care of it first thing in the morning," Tom said.

His father looked at him, met his eyes, and nodded. He said nothing. Then he walked out of the kitchen. Tom thought he heard him sobbing, but he couldn't be sure.

Tom would have bet that, knowing what he had to do, thinking about it would keep him awake all night. But that didn't happen. He was asleep within a minute after he lay down. And the next morning he slept later than he normally did on Saturdays. Usually, when he didn't have to get up at all, he woke up early.

This Saturday was different. It was a quarter to nine when he woke up. He wondered if, somehow, he had stayed

164

asleep to avoid what he was going to have to do when he woke up.

He got out of bed and dressed quietly and went downstairs on tiptoes. He would get Precious out of the library and put him in the Mustang before his parents woke up.

But he heard noise in the kitchen, and when he went into it, he found his father. Precious was gulping down breakfast from his bowl in the corner. Tom and his father exchanged glances, but neither of them spoke.

Tom sat down at the kitchen table and waited for Precious to finish eating. When he had finished, Precious walked over to him and put his head in Tom's lap to have his ears scratched.

"Come on, Precious," Tom said, his voice breaking. "Let's go for a ride."

Precious, who knew what that meant, went to the kitchen door and sat down. He had grown used to the idea that when he went outside, he had to have his muzzle put on first. He waited patiently until Tom had strapped it on him and then gave Tom his paw.

Tom opened the door.

"So long, Precious," Dr. Lockwood said, and then turned his face away.

Tom opened the passenger door of the Mustang and rolled down the window. Precious liked to ride with his head out of the window.

Then he got behind the wheel, backed out of the driveway, and drove to the Veterinary Medicine building at the university. Precious recognized the place, and refused to go inside. Tom had forgotten to bring a leash, and Precious gave him a hard time as Tom dragged him into the building by his collar.

Finally, however, once he was inside the door, he seemed to understand that he had no choice and stopped bracing his feet. Obediently, if reluctantly, he followed Tom down the corridor, into the elevator, and then down the hall to Dr. Harte's office.

"I've got to see Dr. Harte right away," Tom said to the secretary.

"I'm sorry, Tom," she said. "He won't be in until Monday."

"But I thought he always came in on Saturday morning," Tom replied.

"Usually, but he's out of town. He went to a seminar in New Orleans. Is there something wrong?"

"I've got to put Precious down," Tom said. "He attacked my father last night."

"Oh, Tom!" Dr. Harte's secretary said. "I'm so sorry. But there's nobody here who could . . ."

"Okay," Tom said. "Thanks, anyway. I'll take care of it."

By the time he got to the elevator, he had to face the fact that he had no idea how he was going to "take care of it." He had simply presumed that Dr. Harte would be available when he needed him.

Back in the car, he sat for a moment and thought it through. Dr. Harte was not the only veterinarian in town, just the only one they knew. There were all kinds of vets. Ellen Watson was a vet. But he couldn't ask her to put Precious down. She loved him as much as anyone did. It would be a rotten thing for him to ask.

The solution to the problem, clearly, was to go to another vet, one he didn't know, one who didn't know Precious. Just tell him to put Precious down and get it over with. He didn't know what veterinarians charged to kill dogs, but he didn't think it would be more than the sixty-odd dollars he had in his wallet—the fifty his father had given him and the fifteen he'd won playing nine-ball, less what he'd spent bowling and eating and renting the pool table. There was enough money.

He started the car and drove until he found a telephone

booth. He went inside and looked up veterinarians in the yellow pages. He found the address of one three blocks from the phone booth. He drove there and waited for an hour and a quarter until it was his turn. Precious lay on the floor with his head on Tom's foot.

Finally, it was Tom's turn. The veterinarian heard him out and then said he was sorry, but he just couldn't put Precious down unless Tom brought one of his parents in with him.

"My father's in no condition to come here, and my mother's in shock because of what happened last night," Tom said.

"I'm sorry," the veterinarian said, politely but firmly. "There's nothing I can do for you. Wait a couple of days, until one of your parents is feeling better, and then he or she can bring the animal back for destruction."

Tom didn't say thank you, or even good-bye, to the veterinarian. He was afraid that if he opened his mouth, he would say something he would later regret.

He got back in the car again. Precious, enormously relieved that nothing unpleasant had happened to him in a place that smelled like the small animal hospital at the university, put his head on Tom's lap.

The odds were, Tom decided, that any other vet would behave like this one. They would all refuse to put Precious down because Tom was a teen-ager and his parents weren't with him.

Then he thought of a solution. He wondered if he would be able to go through with it. And then he decided he would have to go through with it. Precious had to be put down now. It would have been easier if he could have had Dr. Harte do it, but that just hadn't worked out. He would sneak into the house, go to the gun cabinet, get a shotgun, and take Precious out in the woods and do it.

His father caught him sneaking into the house. "Is it done?" his father asked.

"Dr. Harte's in New Orleans," Tom said. "I went to another vet and he wouldn't do it. So I'm going to do it."

"What do you mean by that?" his father asked.

"I mean I'm going to take the Winchester model twelve and do it," Tom said, his voice breaking.

His father looked at him for a long moment before he replied. "No," he said. "I'll do it. You drive the car, and I'll do it."

"I can do it by myself," Tom said.

"Yeah, you can," his father said. "But I would have to look at my face in the mirror every day from now on, and I couldn't handle that. We'll do it together."

Tom knew there was no sense arguing with his father.

"I'll get the model twelve," his father said. "And we can have this done before your mother wakes up."

They were starting out the kitchen door when a car came up the driveway.

"Who the hell can that be?" Dr. Lockwood asked impatiently.

It was Ellen Watson.

She got out of the car and looked at them, and saw the shotgun. She reached into the back of her car and took out a leather satchel. Then she walked up to them.

"You won't need the shotgun," she said. "Put it up."

"I guess you know what's going on?" Dr. Lockwood asked.

"Dr. Harte's secretary called me," she said, "as soon as Tom left. I got here as quickly as I could."

"You don't want to do this," Tom said.

"I don't like to do it," Ellen Watson said, "but I'm a doctor of veterinary medicine, and a vet takes an oath to prevent suffering in sick animals. Go get him, Tom."

Tom went down the driveway and got Precious out of the Mustang. He got away from Tom and ran up the driveway to greet his friend Ellen Watson.

When Tom got into the kitchen, the kitchen table had

already been cleared off. "You better pick him up, Tom," Ellen Watson said. "Your father can't do it with his hand."

Tom, who could barely see through the tears in his eyes, picked up Precious and set him on the kitchen table.

"I'll hold him," Dr. Lockwood said, pushing Tom gently aside. Tom saw Ellen with a hypodermic syringe in her hand. She put her face close to Precious's chest. Tom wiped his eyes. When he could focus them again, he saw that Precious had decided to lie down on the table.

"I don't have any experience with this sort of thing," Dr. Lockwood said, keeping his voice under control with a terrible effort. "How long does it take?"

"Precious is gone," Ellen Watson said.

"Gone?"

"What we use," Ellen said, also having trouble controlling her voice, "is a chemical that upsets the body chemistry. It works almost instantly. The only thing Precious felt was the prick of the needle."

Tom looked at her in surprise. There were tears running down her cheeks. And then he looked at his father. His father at that instant lost the battle to keep his emotions hidden. He began to sob, as he gently petted Precious's head for the last time.

CHAPTER 17

AFTER ELLEN WATSON HAD LEFT, DR. LOCKWOOD turned to the practical problem of what to do with Precious's body. He was not going to turn him over to the university for incineration with other dead animals.

They put Precious into the station wagon and drove to a piece of land Dr. Lockwood owned in the country. Tom dug a grave in the sandy soil and lowered Precious onto the expensive dog mattress he had refused to sleep on, wrapped it over him, and then covered him up.

On the way home Dr. Lockwood said, "We are going to tell your mother simply that we had Precious put down and that you and I buried him. And then I don't want his name or the word *dog* mentioned again. I can't go through that sort of experience again."

"I'll never want another dog," Tom said. And at that moment he meant it.

Without Precious the house was like a tomb.

"That damned dog is haunting us," Dr. Lockwood said. "I keep seeing him waiting for me at the foot of the stairs. Every time I open the bathroom door, he growls at me."

"I thought we were forbidden to talk about him," Tom said.

"I don't see where talking about him hurts. Just don't even suggest getting another one."

Three months after Precious had died, Dr. Lockwood made his first trip to the plant. Tom met him at the airport when he came back. When they turned off the road to home, Dr. Lockwood asked where they were going.

"There's something I want to show you," Tom said, and drove him to a house in a residential section on the other side of town.

"Who lives here?" Dr. Lockwood said.

"Come on, I'll introduce you," Tom said, and got out of the car. Dr. Lockwood, grumbling, followed him into the house.

Tom introduced his father to the Davenports, a gray-haired, ruddy-faced couple in their late sixties. Dr. Lockwood was obviously confused until Mr. Davenport pushed open the swinging door to his kitchen and motioned Dr. Lockwood through it.

A Labrador bitch growled deep in her throat at this potential threat to her puppies.

"You shouldn't have done this, Tom," Dr. Lockwood said firmly, even angrily.

"That's Princess Irene of Dunway," Tom said. "She was bred in Maine."

Princess Irene didn't regard Tom as a threat to her puppies. She wagged her tail as Tom picked up a male.

"His father's from California," Tom said. "There's no way he can be inbred."

"I told you, no more dogs," Dr. Lockwood said firmly.

"Yeah, I remember," Tom said. "There are champions on both sides, both lines," Tom went on. "This little guy is worth a bundle of money."

He thrust the puppy at his father, who had no choice but to take him.

The puppy yelped.

Dr. Lockwood looked at Mr. Davenport. "Will you take a check?" he asked.

P O S T S C R I P T

THIS BOOK IS DEDICATED WITH LOVE AND respect to my son John, who, when he was sixteen, met his responsibility to put down the family pet in circumstances very much like those described in this book.

And, with fond memories, to Baron Boris Korsky-Rimsakov, the one-hundred-twenty-five-pound Old English sheepdog who gave our family a lot of love before mental illness, the result of inbreeding, got the best of him.

Also, I would like to express my gratitude to Albert V. Corte, D.V.M., who made a valiant effort to help Boris through surgical and other means, and to Fritz Crane, D.V.M., who eventually reached the painful conclusion that the best way to help Boris was by putting him down. Both of these distinguished and dedicated veterinarians went far beyond the call of duty in treating Boris and trying to ease his family's suffering.